The Mercie Collection

SHARON SROCK

THE WOMEN OF VALLEY VIEW SERIES

Callie
Terri
Pam
Samantha
Kate
Karla

DEDICATION

The three stories that make up this collection are gratefully dedicated to my street team. Word of mouth is an author's best friend. These women read, review, and share my stories with their friends. So in no particular order, ladies I appreciate you!!

Amie Tiger
Anne Ellison
Carrie Gould
Janice Sisemore
Sharee Stover
Karen C. Riley
Mary Cordle
Linda Rainey
Amy Campbell
Lynn Beck
Teresa Tallbot
Sharon Dean
Melissa Lemaire
Vicki Marney
Cheri Swalwell
Juanita Wickey
Carol Elle
Becky Hrivnak
Katrina Epperson
Paige Todd
Anne Rightler

FOR MERCIE'S SAKE

CHAPTER ONE

The baby in Scottlyn Rich's womb turned a summersault. She frowned when a tiny foot made painful contact with her bladder. *Easy baby.* Scottlyn followed the principal of Eden Heights Christian Academy down a deserted hall while the baby continued to squirm. *Can she feel how nervous I am?* And if she could, shouldn't they both be used to it by now? The last few months had turned her present and her future upside down. How could anyone go from popular and secure to pregnant and outcast in so short a time and not feel lost? She shrugged and tried to pull her attention back to the guided tour.

The school was bigger than she'd expected. Muffled sounds of classes in session reached her ears as they passed by closed doors. Hand drawn pictures and childishly scribbled assignments hung on bulletin boards outside of each room. The tile floors were scuffed, the metal lockers scratched and dented. Some of the tension between Scottlyn's shoulder blades eased. Eden Heights looked a lot like the public schools she'd always attended.

The principal led her up a short flight of stairs, and somewhere between the first and second floors, they crossed an invisible line from childish to young adult. Good-bye crayon drawings, hello sports schedules, pep squad notices, and social event flyers.

Not what I expected. The idea of attending a Christian

high school had given Scottlyn pause. Church had never been a part of her life, and now? Well...*I might as well paint a red A on my forehead.* She had enough going on in her life without becoming the target for some well-meaning do-gooder. The baby tumbled again. She shifted the load of textbooks in her arms and placed a calming hand on her belly. "Settle down, Mercie."

The principal paused with a half turn. "I'm sorry. Did you have a question?"

A sick heat built in Scottlyn's throat. She jerked to a stop. The books hit the floor as she slapped a hand over her mouth. "Bathroom?"

Principal Hatter frowned at her. "What?" Reality dawned on the woman's face. "Oh my." She pointed.

Scottlyn sprinted down the hall, shoved through the door of the blessedly deserted...*thank God*... restroom, and pushed into a stall. Her stomach emptied as her heart filled with humiliation. Once the retching passed, she leaned against the wall and fumbled for a handful of tissue. She wiped her mouth with trembling hands, wincing when she heard the door swing open followed by the principal's voice.

"Are you OK, dear?"

Wonderful. The perfect start to her first day in a strange place. *I hate this whole thing!* The baby kicked. Scottlyn rubbed the mound of her five-month belly. *Not you, baby.* She continued to rub, inhaling deep breaths and expelling them though her mouth. The trembling subsided. The nausea passed. With a final cleansing breath, she opened the stall. Principal Hatter leaned against the row of sinks, her arms full of Scottlyn's books.

Scottlyn crossed to one of the sinks, turned the tap on, scooped a hand full of water into her mouth, and tried to swish away the remnants of her breakfast. She ripped a paper towel free, blotted her face, and dried her hands.

"You poor thing. Is there anything I can do to help?"

Scottlyn shook her head. "I'll be fine now that my stomach is empty. Sorry."

"You don't have to apologize. I carried three babies. I know how quickly nausea can sneak up on you."

She shrugged. "Thanks. These days, I don't even know what to blame it on. The whole court thing looming over my head, being kicked out by my dad, or Mercie."

"Mercy?"

Her hand went back to her stomach. "My daughter, Mercie. M.E.R.C.I.E."

"What a lovely and unusual name for a baby girl." The principal straightened, shifting the stack of books from her right arm to her left. "I know this is a difficult time for you, but I admire your decisions. I'm here for you if you feel the need to talk. I'm sure your teachers will make themselves available as well. Are you ready to meet your first hour teacher?"

Scottlyn nodded and reached for the books.

Mrs. Hatter swung them out of her reach. "I'll carry them for you." She used her free hand to dig a slip of paper from her pocket. "I have your locker number right here. We'll drop your books off on the way to Mrs. Kensington's classroom."

"Thanks." Scottlyn pasted a smile on her face and squared her shoulders. She'd missed school, the routine, and the learning. She'd always been a good student, and she'd continue to be. Her future, and Mercie's, depended on it.

~ * ~

Diana Kensington closed her eyes against the everyday

noise of her first hour class settling in for the morning. The sound of chairs scraping the floor, the clatter of books landing on desk tops, and the chatter of perky morning voices penetrated her sleep deprived brain like fingernails on a chalkboard.

Resigned, she embraced the four hundred and thirty-ninth day of her new normal with all the enthusiasm of a death row inmate. Another sunrise clutching Chuck's pillow to her chest, hoping for a whiff of his cologne while she searched for the will to crawl out of bed. Another day when her food tasted like straw and her clothes threatened to fall from her rapidly shrinking frame. Another night with nothing to look forward to except endless tossing when she should have been sleeping. Four hundred thirty-nine days since her husband kissed her good bye and spoke the last words she'd ever hear him utter.

"I'm out of here, Blondie."

"Two days?"

"I'll be back in time to take you to dinner Friday night."

Except he didn't come back. Diana's eyes darted to the ceiling as her focus shifted. Now she concentrated on God, the God she'd taken an emotional step away from on the day Chuck's plane fell out of the sky. The words she whispered not meant for anyone's ears but His. "If I'd known, I'd have cooked him breakfast. I'd have told him I loved him. I'd have held on and not let go. I couldn't have known, but *You* knew."

She bowed her head into her hands, pressing her fingers against her eyes, struggling against tears of hopelessness. Not here, not now. Her class deserved better. Her class. A room filled with other people's children. She sucked in a ragged breath as that reminder threatened to steal her resolve. Chuck was gone, and there was nothing in his place. Other women in her situation had children or grandchildren to help fill the void. She had nothing, nothing but an empty house that no longer felt like a home.

The nine o'clock bell rang, forcing her back to the present. She stood as the room shuffled into silence. "OK guys, let's break out those history books. We have a lot of ground to cover before our big test on Wednesday."

Eden Heights was a private school with small classes, twenty-four students max for any subject or classroom. She taught English, History, and Algebra I to both Sophomores and Juniors. Today's lesson on the Revolutionary War was a favorite and should serve to distract her from her gloomy thoughts this morning.

She walked back and forth in front of the twenty students in her class. "Who can tell me where the Constitution was signed?" Several hands went up. "Monica?"

Before Monica could deliver her answer, the door to her room swung open to admit Principal Hatter. Following in the principal's wake was a young girl with a pale, heart shaped face, long blonde hair, and striking blue eyes.

"Sorry to interrupt you, Mrs. Kensington, but I have a new student for you." She paused, motioning the girl to her side. "This is Scottlyn Rich. Scottlyn, this is Mrs. Kensington. She teaches our junior English and History classes, so you'll have her for first and last hour."

Diana took a step forward with her hand outstretched. Scottlyn did the same, shuffling a textbook, notebook, and purse in the process. Diana froze, her eyes locked on the newly exposed bulge around the girl's middle. *Pregnant?* Teacher and student exchanged a weak handshake.

Diana struggled to keep her smile in place. She nodded to an empty desk. "Have a seat." She looked at Principal Hatter. "Could we have a word?"

Millicent Hatter nodded and led the way into the deserted hallway. Diana pulled the door closed behind them.

"A pregnant student, Millicent? I thought we had rules about this sort of thing. What's going on here?"

Millicent shook her head. "I'm sorry, Diana. You weren't here Friday when I talked to the other teachers. I don't want to take your class time to explain, and I have an appointment right after work. If you'll stop by my office before class starts in the morning, I'll share the details with you." She placed a hand on Diana's shoulder. "Trust me, I was hesitant at first, but once I heard the whole story and took some time to pray about the situation, I knew we had to offer Scottlyn a chance."

Diana watched Millicent walk away. Tension born of resentment lay heavy on her neck and shoulders. Could this day get any more tedious? She turned to re-enter her class and stopped with her hand on the knob. A single prayer escaped her lips for the four hundred and thirty-ninth day in a row. "What now, God?"

CHAPTER TWO

Sabor, Oklahoma, didn't offer many dining choices. Folks looking for fast food could choose between a taco, a burger, a pizza, or a sub sandwich. All national chains, with every bite as predictable as the sun rising in the east. The town's idea of fine dining wasn't much better. Sabor's six-block main street offered Mexican, Italian, Chinese, and one mom-and-pop that served everything and specialized in nothing.

Diana pulled open the door to Rosita's, waved at the hostess behind the register, and slid into a booth next to the window. The spicy aroma of peppers and onions drifted in from the kitchen, hanging in the air in a tantalizing combination. It should have stirred her appetite. *Not so much.* She and Lynette had a standing Monday night dinner date, her friend's obvious attempt to make sure she ate at least one decent meal a week. A plan that failed more often than it succeeded.

She struggled to relax, but every time the stress began to fade, a picture of her new student formed in her memory. *Why?* Why were irresponsible girls, with no experience, fewer resources, and even less desire to mother a child granted the thing she'd been denied?

She chafed, reminded of the years and money spent trying to fill her useless womb. She should be too old to care, but girls like Scottlyn Rich seemed to mock her for what she would never have.

The bell above the door chimed as it swung open, admitting Lynette Thomas. How did her friend always look so fresh after a day spent behind the appointment desk of a pediatric clinic? And how she walked at the end of the day in those three inch heels was another mystery. Lynette's teal blouse complimented her ebony skin. The matching handkerchief skirt teased the calves of her legs as she glided across the floor to the booth. Diana rose to receive a quick kiss to her cheek, Lynette's traditional greeting.

Lynette slid into the bench seat across from Diana. She leaned forward, planted an elbow on the table, and braced her chin in her hand. Diana squirmed under the intense study. Lynette finally shook her head.

"Down another pound since yesterday, I'll bet. Girlfriend, if you don't start eating, I'm going to haul your skinny butt over to the clinic and start you on a protein IV."

"There's no such thing."

"I'll get the doc to make one up special." Lynette shook her head. "Seriously, Diana, you can't afford to lose any more weight."

It was a months-old argument. "I've always wanted to be svelte."

Lynette narrowed her chocolate eyes.

"All right, already. I'm working on it. I had breakfast *and* lunch today." To prove her increased appetite, Diana plucked a chip from the basket resting in the center of the table and nibbled a corner. It tasted like cardboard.

"You're not fooling me with that act. Let me guess...four bites of corn flakes this morning and a small bag of chips at lunch."

"A half bowl of cereal and one of those cans of

microwavable tomato soup," Diana countered.

"Oh wow. Keep eating like that, and we'll be letting out your clothes in a week." The waitress approached for their order, and Lynette paused her scolding to study the menu. "What comes with the child's taco plate?"

"One taco plus rice and beans."

"Great. I'll have the adult sized taco dinner and bring the child sized one for my friend here." The waitress nodded and hurried away. Lynette turned her attention back to Diana. "You're eating everything on that plate before we leave this table."

"I'm not a five-year-old."

"Could have fooled me."

A wolf whistle sounded from the depths of Lynette's oversized tote. Diana noted the time. Five thirty on the dot. Lynette's husband worked the swing shift, and he called her every evening on his first break, just to say hello. Her friend had no idea how lucky she was.

Girl talk went on hold while Lynette dug through the tote bag for her phone. A folded newspaper, a worn new testament, sunglasses, and a bulging cosmetic bag landed in a heap on the table before she found it. One of the newspaper headlines captured Diana's attention. She slid the paper over to get a better look while her friend talked to her husband.

Local college quarterback pleads guilty to rape charges.

Diana opened the paper wider to read the story. The piece offered only the stingiest of details regarding the rape of a sixteen-year-old girl by a Sabor High graduate. "That poor child."

Lynette looked up. "What?"

Diana shook her head and bent to read more of the story.

"Have a good night. Love you too." Lynette dropped

the phone back into her bag. "What's got you mumbling?"

Diana flattened the paper on the table between them. She tapped the article. "This. Sixteen years old, and her life is ruined. It's just sad."

"I can't believe you're just now seeing this. It's been in the news for weeks."

Diana shrugged. "I don't get into the news much. Chuck always read the paper and shared the highlights with me. Now, I catch snips of the national news when I'm on-line for something."

"You need to tune back into the world, Diana. This whole thing between Bradley Nelson and..." Lynette paused and snapped her fingers softly. "...oh, what *is* her name? Stephanie...Shelia...Scottlyn. That's it! This whole thing between Bradley Nelson and Scottlyn is unfolding in your own backyard."

Diana gasped at the name. *Please, God let there be two of them.* "Scottlyn?"

"Scottlyn Rich. Do you know her?"

Diana's heart lodged in her throat. "I do now. She enrolled at Eden Heights today." She took a drink. "She was raped?"

Lynette replaced the contents of her bag, waiting while the waitress positioned hot, fragrant plates on the table. She studied Diana through the steam. "Yes. I'll tell you what I know if you promise to eat while I talk."

"Deal." Diana picked up her taco. "I want the whole story." She bit into the taco and chewed, waiting for Lynette to do the same.

Lynette swallowed and took a sip of her Diet Coke. "Well, according to the clinic grape vine and my very nosey next door neighbor, Scottlyn Rich, a member of Sabor High's band, accepted an invitation to a nearby university to check out scholarship possibilities. The trip included four other promising members of the band and came with the opportunity to spend the weekend in the dorms. A slice of college life, if you will." She paused for another bite of taco and a fork full of refried beans. She motioned to Diana's plate. "Eat, or I'm done."

Diana frowned across the table, but she scooped rice and beans onto a chip and followed it with another bite of her taco.

"Scottlyn Rich claims, and testimony from the other four students verifies, that they were invited to a coed mixer on the Saturday night of their visit. What can't be verified by witnesses is the Rich girl's claim that she was raped by the college's up-and-coming quarterback, a former Sabor High player being groomed to take the place of the current quarterback, who's graduating this spring." Lynette dipped a chip into melted cheese. "The news today claims that a second victim stepped forward at the last minute. The young man in question accepted a plea bargain in exchange for a reduced sentence rather than facing a jury trial."

"Scottlyn's pregnancy is the result of the rape?"

"That's the story."

Diana sat back, the taco she'd consumed formed an ugly lump in her stomach. *Judgmental, stupid...idiot!* "Terrific."

"Excuse me?"

"I wasn't exactly thrilled to have her in my class. I voiced my *concerns* to Millicent Hatter, who'd like to see me before class in the morning." Diana closed her eyes and leaned her head against the back of the booth. "There is no way that child failed to notice my negative attitude."

"You didn't know."

"And what difference does that make, really? This

poor kid didn't do anything wrong, and even if she had, we're Christians, taught to love the sinner in spite of the sin." Diana sat up. "How she got into the condition she's in shouldn't affect the way I treat her."

Lynette nodded, sympathy evident in her eyes.

Diana was tired of people's sympathy. She stared into the distance beyond the booth while she chewed. "Have I become so bitter that I can't see beyond my own grief?"

She needs your help.

Diana smirked even as the words formed in her heart. "How can I help her when I can't help myself?"

"What?"

She shook herself out of her daze. "Nothing...just...thinking out loud."

Lynette shrugged and popped the last of her taco into her mouth. "What are you going to do?"

"Well, first I need to apologize for the way I behaved. Beyond that..."

She needs your help.

Diana shrugged. "Besides being the best teacher I can be, I don't have anything to offer her."

Lynette shook her head. "You need to stop selling yourself so short...Would you look at that."

"What?"

Lynette motioned to Diana's plate. "You ate it all."

Diana looked down at her empty plate. Child's plate or not, it was the first full meal she'd eaten since Chuck's death. "I was coerced."

"Maybe. Or maybe you just needed something to take your mind off your own problems."

~ * ~

Scottlyn rolled from her side to her back. The twin-sized mattress was lumpy, and the thin sheets didn't actually fit, but at least it was a bed. One of five beds crammed into a room more suited for three. The occupants of the other beds, each in some stage of pregnancy, seemed to be sleeping soundly. Even in February, the collective body heat made the space unbearably stuffy. Her sigh sounded loud in the quiet room. Beggars can't be choosers.

She searched for a comfortable position. The movement woke the baby, and Mercie decided to join the late night party. She practiced her cheerleading kicks and stretches while Scottlyn tried to no avail to soothe the active baby with pats and rubs. She needed to walk, but there was no room. She tossed the blankets back, shoved her feet into her slippers and crept out of the room as quietly as possible.

Scottlyn paced the deserted hallway, guided by evenly spaced night-lights. Behind one of the doors a baby cried. She'd seen the rooms for the mothers and newborns. Two beds, two three-drawer chests, and two cribs crammed into each room. All together, the Choose Life Shelter had room for ten unwed mothers and six new mothers and their babies. Thank goodness there'd been an empty bed when she'd needed one. She hoped there'd be an empty mommy bed and crib by the time Mercie arrived.

She counted and mumbled while she walked. "Hillary and Linda's babies are almost six months old. They'll both be out of the mommy rooms long before Mercie gets here. If Val gives up her baby and goes home like she said she would, then even if Tammi moves into one of the rooms, I can have the other. Assuming I have my baby before Jessica." She reached the end of the hall and wandered back in the other direction. "But if Jess has hers first, she'll get that room, and what if Amber decides to keep her baby? If there isn't a room available, will they kick me out? Where will I go?" Her head ached with the *what ifs,* and she lifted her hands to massage her temples. "This is all just so hard!"

Scottlyn stopped in a stingy circle of light cast by one of the small bulbs. Her shadow loomed on the wall, and she turned to study her profile. She molded her oversized T-shirt to the ever growing bulge around her middle. "I'm going to be a mommy." The words warmed her heart and chilled her soul at the same time. Was she ready? Could she be a good mother when she had no idea how a good mother acted? "Don't worry, baby, we'll figure it out together. I promise that you'll never have to wonder if I love you, or why I didn't want to keep you. I'll never leave you like my mom left me." Thoughts of a mother she couldn't remember sent a tear streaking down her cheek. How could she miss someone she'd never known? She brushed the tear aside. "Stupid hormones!" she hissed into the silence.

The stairs leading to the floor above her creaked, followed by a loud whisper. "Who's down there?"

"Scottlyn." She stepped to the base of the staircase and peered into the gloom. One of the house parents looked down at her. "The baby was restless, so I was walking." And talking to herself like a crazy person. "Sorry if I bothered you."

"No bother, sweetheart. Just making sure everyone's OK. No one's due this week, but babies keep their own schedules. Come get me if you need anything."

"Thanks, I will, but I think we can sleep now." She retreated to the end of the hall and crept back into her bed. It was going to be OK. Bradley had admitted to the rape. For now, she had a roof over her head and plenty to eat, and Eden Heights offered her the chance to continue her education. Mrs. Hatter was a sweetheart. She'd been beyond kind today. *Mrs. Kensington doesn't like me much.* Scottlyn shrugged. Mrs. Kensington would have to suck it up and get over it.

Scottlyn was determined to accomplish two things. She would keep her baby, and she would have her education. Teachers, parents, or whoever else had issues with her decisions could all take a flying leap.

SHARON SROCK

CHAPTER THREE

Diana followed Millicent into the small corner office. She closed the door as the principal crossed to the coffee maker perched atop a filing cabinet.

"Coffee?"

Diana shook her head. "Not the best beverage to have with a large helping of crow."

Millicent turned and regarded Diana through the steam hovering over her cup. "Crow?" She circled to her desk and took her seat.

"I had a long talk with a friend last night. I know Scottlyn isn't the typical pregnant teen." She raised a hand before Millicent could speak. "And before you remind me, I understand that even if she were, it's not my place to judge." She'd thought of little besides Scottlyn since dinner the night before. When Chuck was still alive, Diana had been one of those teachers all the kids knew they could count on, compassionate, kind, and helpful. Now...? Well, her reaction to that pregnant teenager made her wonder—had she become too bitter to be compassionate? The answer made her bite her lip. "I was startled when you brought her into my classroom. In the ten years I've taught here, we've never admitted a pregnant student."

Millicent nodded. "That has been our policy, and it will continue to be our policy with this one exception."

She paused to take a sip from her cup. "Are you familiar with the Choose Life Shelter?"

Diana shook her head.

"I didn't think so. We're just getting off the ground. Choose Life is a home for unwed mothers. I haven't shared this with many people, but I'm a member of their board. When the principal of Scottlyn's former school called me for help, I knew I had to act, and I knew that my decision probably wouldn't be very popular."

The aroma wafting from the coffee pot ignited a rarely felt desire. "May I change my mind about a cup of coffee?" Principal Hatter nodded, and Diana rose to prepare a cup. "Whether or not your decision is popular isn't the point. Women...girls have babies. That's not something we've tried to keep from our students. But even though this is a special case, I worry about the message we're sending here." Diana shrugged. "I'm glad the decision is yours and not mine."

Principal Hatter motioned Diana back to her seat. "Let me tell you a story." Millicent settled into her chair and cupped her hands around her mug. "A young girl, a promising musician, attended a mixer hosted by the college she hoped to attend in a couple of years. During that mixer she grew bored with the noise and decided to walk, alone, back to the dormitory where she was spending the night. As she was leaving, a handsome young football player, a graduate from her high school, someone whose name she recognized and trusted, offered to walk with her. She accepted his offer of kindness, only to find out that kindness was not his motivation."

She paused to enjoy a taste of her coffee. "She was hurt and angry and embarrassed at her own 'stupidity' and allowed the rape to go unreported until, six weeks later, she realized she was pregnant. She went to her father, expecting support, and explained everything. Her father pushed for immediate and justifiable legal action. He also demanded she have an abortion."

Diana gasped at the word.

Millicent nodded. "Sad but true. The father did not want his daughter, or himself, *saddled* with a product of rape."

"Oh, bless her heart."

"There's more." Millicent abandoned the pretense of her story. "When Scottlyn refused to have an abortion, her father pushed her toward adoption. She could have the baby if she must, but she would not bring it into his house. During this time, the young football player, a graduate of Sabor High, was arrested and charged. The school became a place divided. The accused and the victim both have friends there. The accused also has younger twin brothers in Scottlyn's class. Brothers who, despite the young man's confession last week, are incensed because Scottlyn ruined their brother's scholarship and his dreams for the future."

Diana nodded. "So you accepted her here."

"Both here and at Choose Life."

"The shelter you mentioned. But her parents...?"

"Kicked her out. And it's just a father making these decisions. Scottlyn's mother abandoned her family when Scottlyn was a baby. Mr. Rich is perfectly willing to welcome his daughter home after the baby is born and placed for adoption."

"That poor child."

"Puts a different perspective on the situation, doesn't it? And yes, I know this sends a message—choosing to do the right thing in the face of adversity. This isn't a Christian family, Diana. Scottlyn has no religious training to base her decisions on. All she has is strength, compassion, mercy..." The principal paused, tilted her head, and stared at the wall.

"Millicent?"

Millicent shook her head and focused bright eyes on Diana. "Scottlyn's baby is a girl. She told me she was planning to name her daughter Mercie. There's a certain poetic justice in that, don't you think?"

~ * ~

Diana strolled the aisles of her classroom as her students focused on their reading assignment. She stopped here and there to answer a whispered question. The test tomorrow would count as twenty-five percent of their third quarter grade. Most of the class took that seriously. The dismissal bell rang, putting an abrupt end to the silence of the study period. Diana stepped to the door.

"Ladies and gentlemen, any questions before you leave?" She waited as feet shuffled and heads shook. "Good enough." She swung the door open. "I'll see you tomorrow. Scottlyn, could I have a word with you before you go?"

Scottlyn sank back into her chair. Diana closed the door behind the last student. She'd left this until the end of the day, hoping they could talk without feeling rushed. She returned to her desk and leaned against the corner in what she hoped was a casual pose. Guilt tugged at her heart when the teen refused to meet her gaze. *No more than I deserve.*

"Scottlyn, are you comfortable taking this test tomorrow?"

The girl's response was a whisper. "Yes, ma'am."

"Are you sure? I don't have a problem doing a makeup test after you've had a couple of weeks to catch up."

Scottlyn raised her eyes. Diana saw defiance edged with determination in the blue orbs. "I don't need special treatment." The gleam of tears replaced the defiance. "All I want to do is finish school and raise my child. Why is everyone making that so hard?" She bowed her head and shuffled the books on the desktop. "Sorry. I'll take the test tomorrow. It'll be fine. I was only out of school for a week, and you guys are a little behind what we were doing at SHS."

Diana moved from the corner of the desk to pull one of the student chairs over to Scottlyn's desk. She sat, mulled over the best way to proceed, and decided on simplicity. "I'm sorry." The silence she received in response didn't come as much of a surprise. "Scottlyn, please look at me."

The teenager raised her head, shook blonde hair out of her face, and crossed her arms atop her swollen middle. The blue gaze swept across Diana before coming to rest on the wall over her right shoulder.

"I reacted badly yesterday. Part of that was surprise. I've taught here for ten years. We've never had a pregnant student. I'll admit the rest was both personal and judgmental." Her shoulders lifted in a quick shrug. "You don't deserve either." She held out her hand and saw Scottlyn's eyes flick in that direction for the briefest second. "I'm willing to start fresh if you'll give me a chance." Diana's hand remained suspended and ignored while the seconds ticked by.

~ * ~

Scottlyn stared at Mrs. Kensington's hand. A true apology? Or was she being patronized? Why was it so impossible for people to see her side of things? She never asked to be sixteen and pregnant. Never gave it a thought until that stupid test came back blue. That blue plus sign had burned into her memory as if branded there by a hot iron. *All of my hopes and dreams changed that day.* The baby stirred, and she laid a hand over the movement. *You became my life that day, Mercie.* My life, *not someone to be aborted, or given away, or apologized for.* Her words came out in a barely audible whisper. "I'm tired of being judged. I didn't do anything wrong."

Mrs. Kensington leaned closer. "What did you say?"

She shook herself out of her internal battle. It was a never-ending loop of questions, what-if's, and should haves. The teacher's hand remained outstretched. Scottlyn reached out to clasp it in her own. "Sorry, I seem to stay a little distracted these days." She gave the hand a quick shake before continuing. "My name is Scottlyn Denise Rich. I like to read. The only thing I love more than books is music. I play the flute, and I'm an A student."

Scottlyn shrugged when Mrs. Kensington sat back with a puzzled expression. "You said you wanted to start fresh. That's the best introduction I could come up with on short notice."

The teacher crossed her arms and studied Scottlyn, her lips twitching in a half smile. "You left out the part about having a quick sense of humor and a delightful smile."

"Yeah well, those things are a little rusty these days. I..." Her stomach growled loudly, and her cheeks burned. She covered her face with her hands and peeked out through splayed fingers. "Sorry, my sense of humor might be rusty, but my stomach is getting plenty of exercise." Scottlyn lowered her hands and looked down at her belly. "She's little, but she's always hungry."

"You know what?" Mrs. Kensington paused, a puzzled

look on her face. "So am I."

Why would she sound so surprised to be hungry?

"Do you have someplace to be?"

Weird. Scottlyn shrugged. "Not really, just back to the shelter for dinner and a couple of hours of homework before bed. I'm usually a zombie by eight thirty these days. Why?"

CHAPTER FOUR

"Turn left here."

Diana followed Scottlyn's directions, coming to a stop at the curb in front of a sprawling old house. Three stories tall, it crouched on the tree-covered lot and loomed over the deserted gravel road. Scaffolding marched up the outside walls, evidence of ongoing renovations. Evenly spaced windows spilled light from all three floors and softened the imposing appearance of the structure.

"Wow, this is quite a place. I've lived in Sabor most of my life, but I never knew this beautiful old house existed."

"It's sort of off the beaten path."

"Yes, but..." Diana stopped, squinting through the dusk at the scaffolding. "Still a work in progress, I see."

"Just on the outside. The inside renovations are complete." Scottlyn reached for the door handle. "Anyway, thanks for dinner. The pizza was a treat." She looked back. "You want to come in for a few minutes? I can give you a tour."

"No, it's almost six and I have papers to grade, and you need to spend some time with your history book before our test—"

Go in and let her show you around.

What? Diana looked over her left shoulder, then her

29

right.

Take the tour.

Diana frowned at the house through the windshield. "What on earth...?"

"What did you say?"

Diana jumped at Scottlyn's words, still trying to figure out where those other words had come from. She must've imagined them, but they'd seemed so...real. "Oh...nothing. Better get inside. I'll see you tomorrow." She reached for the gear shift, or at least that was her intention. She suddenly found her entire body weighed down with gravity, like she'd transported to Jupiter. Her arm failed to obey the mental command to move. She slumped into the seat with a confused huff of breath.

"Are you OK?"

"Fine, I'm fine."

Take the tour.

The deep voice rumbled in her heart more than in her ears. "Did you hear that?"

Scottlyn twisted in the seat, looking in every direction. "What?"

Diana shifted to face her student, sighed, and smiled. "I'd love to see the inside of the house." The weighty lethargy vanished the second she moved to release her seatbelt.

"OK," Scottlyn said, dragging out the two syllables in confusion.

The girl led the way up the cracked cement walk. "The tour won't take long. The common rooms are on the first floor, the bedrooms are on the second. The third floor is reserved for staff. We aren't allowed up there unless it's an emergency." She threw the door open and allowed Diana to precede her.

Diana stepped into a spacious foyer with a gleaming

hardwood floor. The ceiling towered over her head, and a sweeping staircase led to the upper floors. Rooms branched off the entry in three directions. "Wow, it looks like a mini version of the Beverly Hillbillies mansion."

"The Beverly who?"

Diana chuckled. "Never mind. It's lovely."

Scottlyn shrugged. "Its home, for now anyway." She motioned Diana into the left. "This is our TV room."

Diana took in the cozy grouping of sofas and chairs, along with the flat screen on the north wall. The room was unoccupied at the moment, but she could imagine it filled with female chatter. "Awfully quiet in here. Where is everyone?"

"Most of us are still in school. After dinner is designated study time. We aren't allowed to watch TV until after eight. Those who aren't in school usually hang out in the library to help out with the babies or homework."

"Oh, that's a nice system."

Scottlyn backed out of the room and led her across the hall. The sound of muted voices crept out from under the door. "The library is through there. I'll show you if you want, but I hate to interrupt—"

"Not a problem. We can leave that room off the tour for now."

"It's a really cool place. Think study hall combined with nursery. Nice big tables so you can spread your stuff out without getting in anyone else's way. Lots and lots of books, and portable cribs for the babies. Being a new mom doesn't get you out of studying." They walked down the back hall side by side. "The kitchen and dining area are back here."

Diana caught a glimpse of stainless steel appliances and spotless counter tops as Scottlyn swept her through the kitchen and into a huge dining room. A long wooden table, big enough to accommodate a small army, dominated the space. She counted twenty chairs before her student interrupted her.

"The food here is really good. It's sort of like a big family when we all sit down."

Diana heard a note of wistfulness in the teenager's voice.

Scottlyn cleared her throat and plucked a banana from a bowl on the sideboard. A large coffee pot sat next to the bowl of fruit. "They keep plenty of snacks available too." She patted her belly. "Never know when the munchies are going to strike. But I'd stay away from the coffee." The youngster shuddered. "Decaf, yuck!"

They circled back to the entry hall and climbed the stairs to the second floor. Scottlyn led the way to the first room on the left and threw the door wide. "This is my home sweet home."

The room was huge with lovely high ceilings and decorative crown molding. It should have felt spacious. Instead, five twin-sized beds, three on one wall and two on the other, interspaced with five small chests of drawers, left little more than a narrow aisle down the middle and made the room seem cramped. The only touch of personality came from the things that had been hung on the walls above the beds and arranged on the tops of the chests. There, stuffed animals vied for attention with school books and trophies, along with posters of the latest movie heart throb.

Scottlyn led her to the last bed in the room. "This is mine."

Diana crossed her arms and studied the meager space. No posters there. She took a step closer to examine the pictures taped to the wall above Scottlyn's bed. A small house behind a white picket fence, assorted baby furniture, a shiny red vehicle, and a puppy. "What's all this?"

Scottlyn ducked her head. "It's my wish wall."

"A wish wall?"

"Its pictures of all the things I plan to give my baby someday." Her young face grew determined, and she reached out to touch the picture of the house. "I'm going to make a home for my daughter." Her fingers rested on each picture in turn. "She's going to have a beautiful nursery and a puppy to keep her company."

Diana's breath caught in her lungs when Scottlyn's hand hovered over the picture of her dream car. *Dear God...*

The quiet gasp drew Scottlyn's attention back to Diana. She flashed a sheepish grin. "The car's sort of for both of us. I'll need a job and wheels to get back and forth." She patted the picture. "I want an SUV instead of a car. I've heard they're safer, and I want the best for my baby. I just have to figure out a way to make that happen." Diana had no time to respond before the teenager led her out of the room.

Scottlyn motioned across the hall. "That's another room, just like mine. The last three are the mommy rooms. She paused and knocked on a closed door. When no one answered, she opened the door a crack and peered inside. She flipped on the light and opened the door wider. "I figured everyone was downstairs. This is where the mommies and new babies live."

Diana peeked in to see a smaller room with two neatly made beds, two cribs, and two chests of drawers, twins to the ones in the previous room. "This is quite a set up. How many girls live here?"

"Sixteen. Ten preggies and six mommies."

"Wow." Diana looked around. "That's quite a group. How do you guys keep things so neat?"

"What do you mean?"

"Well, when you've got six little ones running around, I guess I'd expect to see some toys and clutter. I'm impressed that you girls are able to keep everything so tidy."

"Six-month-olds don't make a lot of mess."

"What do you mean?"

"We all have to find a place to live by the time our babies are six months old. House policy."

"But..." Diana did the math in her head. "You'll only be seventeen. You won't even be out of school. What—?"

"I don't know!" Scottlyn closed her eyes, turned her back, and took a few steps away. When she faced Diana again, her eyes were bright with restrained tears. She lifted her hand and took a few deep breaths. "Sorry, but I'm so sick of that question." The hand she raked through her hair shook. "And so tired of not knowing the answer." Her blue eyes dropped to her rounded middle, and she hugged her arms around it protectively. "I didn't know what I was going to do the morning after the...the rape." The last word was a whisper. "I didn't know what I was going to do when the pregnancy test came back positive." She raised her hands in a gesture of surrender. "I didn't know what I was going to do when my father kicked me out of our house. And I don't know what I'll do when my six months are up. But I know I have to make good choices now, because my baby is depending on me. I have to do the right thing for Mercie's sake."

Diana looked into the tear-filled eyes of her new student, and the band of grief wrapped around her soul loosened. As desperate as she'd been, as lost as she'd felt since Chuck's death, she still had so much to be thankful for. She was the teacher, but this child with no concept of Christianity was giving her an education on more than one subject. *Father, I've been blind—and selfish—in my pain. Forgive me.*

Share hope with her.

Diana heard the words and had no doubt of the source. But, how could she offer Scottlyn what she'd abandoned?

How can you not offer her the hope she needs?

Diana shook her head. She needed to put her own house in order before she tried to order someone else's. She reached out to Scottlyn. The youngster clasped her hand and held on like it was a life line. "I know you've felt alone the last few months. I can't imagine what you've gone through. I can't understand how you've stayed so strong. I want you to understand that you've got people on your side now. We're going to help you get through this."

When a sob escaped Scottlyn's throat, Diana's heart broke. "I'm not going to lie to you and tell you things are going to be *fixed* from here on out, but I can promise that you won't face another thing alone." She pulled the girl into a hug. It wasn't the perfect solution, it wasn't the Christian witness she felt compelled to share, but it was all she had at the moment.

~ * ~

Diana paced the kitchen. Each time the circuit led her past the door to the garage, her steps fumbled. *No, no, no...no!* Prayer or argument? Didn't really matter, because the answer was still no.

Daughter, I've watched you grieve for more than a year. It's time to move on.

"You're asking too much."

What have you asked Me every day?

Diana stopped, leaned against the counter, and closed her eyes. Her whispered answer echoed loud in the silence of the empty house. "What now, God?"

This is now.

Warmth encircled her like strong arms, and Diana sobbed into them, allowing the tears to wash away a bit of the hurt and grief of the past months. When the crying jag subsided, she stepped to the garage door and threw it open. She reached in and flipped on the overhead light. Sitting in the middle of the dim space was Chuck's Toyota Rav4. The exact vehicle, identical down to the color and style of the chrome wheels, to the one pictured on Scottlyn's wish wall.

The shiny red SUV was Chuck's last major purchase before his death. Paid for in full by his life insurance. Untouched since he'd left her. Diana wrapped her arms around her body. *Dear God, where are you taking me?*

CHAPTER FIVE

The rest of the week passed uneventfully. Diana went to her job each day, her mind so preoccupied, she taught her lessons on autopilot. She breathed a sigh of relief and pride when all of her students passed the third quarter history test. In her ten years at Eden Heights, that had only happened one other time.

Scottlyn came to school every day, and despite Diana's initial misgivings, Scottlyn and her classmates seemed to be adjusting well to each other. She'd noticed several of the other girls clustered around the pregnant student in the hall on numerous occasions. Animated smiles, whispered conversations, the occasional placement of a new girlfriend's hand against the swell of her belly, all accented by rounded eyes, gasps of surprise, and companionable laughter as Scottlyn shared the wonder of new life with them. Every time Diana's eyes rested on her new student, Scottlyn's words from earlier in the week rang in her ears. "I don't know what I'll do when my six months are up." Each time those words replayed, Diana felt the same nudge in her spirit and fought to resist. If it had just been the car, she could have convinced her heart to let go, but what she felt went light years beyond Chuck's Rav4.

The snoozing Sunday morning alarm sounded for the second time. Diana turned it off, struggled with a yawn, and stretched like a cat beneath the warm cocoon of her blankets. She smiled as a few stiff joints popped. She'd slept like the dead. *That's the first time I've slept that well in...*Her mind reached out to pick up the cross of her daily grief and came up empty. *Wait!* She counted aloud. "Monday...Monday...I remember counting the days on Monday." But today, she couldn't figure out how many it had been since he'd died. It seemed...wrong. *Isn't that being disloyal to Chuck's memory?* Wasn't that letting go of him? She waited for the familiar panic that normally accompanied such thoughts. The only thing her body produced was a growling stomach and a long lost yearning for peanut butter melted on fresh wheat toast.

She pictured an unopened jar of strawberry preserves in the pantry and rolled out of the bed. She tossed the comforter into place and fumbled with her slippers. Toast *and* cereal for breakfast. Lynette would be so proud.

~ * ~

Diana's Sunday school teacher called the class to order. Everyone rushed to refill their coffee or grab a final snack before settling in their seats around the large tables arranged in a U shape in the church's fellowship hall.

Diana set her coffee toward the center of the table and looked at the verses written on the white board. She flipped through her Bible to find the first one.

Movement across the room caught her eye. Jeremy Ripple waved his hand at their teacher. He stood once he had her attention. "I've got something I want to share with the class before we get started. I almost missed out on an important blessing this week." He paused as his voice cracked, smiling at his wife when she passed him a tissue.

Rough and tough Jeremy in tears? Diana leaned forward on her elbows and rested her chin in her hand.

"I took a quick lunch break on Thursday and drove down to the Sonic. When I pulled off the interstate, there was a panhandler leaning against the yield sign with, *Stranded, please help* scribbled on a piece of cardboard." Jeremy wiped his streaming eyes. "We've all seen them, we've all ignored them. It's so hard to tell the truly needy from the simply greedy." He stopped and allowed the chuckles at his joke to dissipate.

He placed a hand on his wife's shoulder before he continued. "I tell Linda to never, ever stop for these people. The world's a dangerous place, and misplaced sympathy isn't worth the risk. Anyway, he was leaning there, and I got the strongest urge to buy him a couple of burgers. I tried to ignore it and go about my business. I parked and ordered my lunch, but by the time it got there, I was nearly too sick to my stomach to eat. I couldn't get his haggard face out of my head. So I ordered two more burgers and a soda and drove back to where he was standing. I barely even stopped. I just rolled down the window, handed the bag through, and then went across the street to that vacant lot everyone uses as a carpool meeting place to eat the lunch I didn't get to eat at the Sonic."

The ragged breath Jeremy sucked in seemed at odds with the smile beaming on his face. "Anyway, this guy starts across the street in my direction. Not towards my car but towards one of the cars parked further back. An older model with a beat up U-haul hitched to the back. He..." Jeremy's voice broke completely, and he stopped to wipe his nose. "He opened the back door, and these two little boys tumbled out and snatched at those burgers like they hadn't seen food in a week. It almost broke my heart. I said a prayer for them, glad I'd listened...figuring I'd finished what God had asked. I was wrong. A Bible verse flooded my mind. James 2:15-16. I want to read it to you." Jeremy stopped and retrieved his Bible from the table, opened it, and removed the sticky note marking his place.

"If a brother or sister be naked, and destitute of daily food, and one of you say unto them, depart in peace, be ye warmed and filled: notwithstanding ye give them not those things which are needful to the body: what doth it profit?" Jeremy closed his Bible and allowed his gaze to roam the room.

Are you listening, daughter?

Diana squirmed and sank down in her seat, trying to take refuge behind her coffee cup when his bright eyes swept in her direction and seemed to linger on her before moving on. Everyone else in the class waited for the rest of the story with sniffles and muffled tears.

"I walked over there and asked the man his name, told him what fine looking boys he had, and asked him if there was anything else I could do for him. His story nearly broke my heart. He told me that he'd lost his wife three years ago and his job six months ago. He had a cousin and a new job waiting on him in Houston, but his car broke down outside of town, and it took all of his cash to get it repaired. Him and his two boys had been sleeping in the car and eating what the Good Lord provided for two days."

Linda held his hand, and Jeremy continued. "I stand by what I said, especially for you ladies. It's just not safe to deal with these people, but sometimes there's this little voice in your head and heart we all need to listen to. This was one of those times for me. I took that family back to the Sonic, fed them a proper lunch, got them food to go for their dinner, and gave him two hundred dollars for his trip. I gave him my phone number and told him to call me if he needed anything else. I got a call last night. They arrived in Houston safe and sound." Jeremy opened his Bible to a second sticky note. "I've got one more verse I want to share, and then I'll sit down and hush.

"Hebrews 13:12 says, "Let brotherly love continue. Be not forgetful to entertain strangers: for there by some have entertained angels unawares.'" He stopped to blow his nose again. "I don't think Adam and his boys were angels, but I'm so glad I took the time to listen to what God was trying to tell me." Jeremy sat down, and the class fiddled with cups, Bibles, and lesson books for a few seconds as everyone processed his story. Finally, the teacher called them to prayer for Adam and his family.

As prayers ascended around her, Diana sank even deeper into her seat. She was happy for Jeremy's testimony, but if she listened to the still small voice in her own heart and obeyed what she felt God wanted her to do, her life would never be the same.

Trust Me, it will be better.

CHAPTER SIX

Scottlyn arranged her pillows against the headboard on Sunday afternoon. She shifted until she found a comfortable spot for both her and the baby. Lunch was over, her homework assignments were complete, and her laundry was done. Downstairs, it was either movie time for those interested or study time for those with weekend homework. For now, she had the bedroom to herself. *It's time for a little* me *time.* She replaced her ear buds, turned on her iPod, and opened her novel. The sounds of the instrumental music combined with the fictional world of the book and offered her a brief escape from the worries of her reality.

She'd managed four whole pages before a knock sounded on the doorframe. She looked up and brushed the ear buds aside. One of the housemothers stood in the opening.

"Scottlyn, you have a visitor. I put him in the dining room, since it's empty for the time being."

She marked her place in the book, laid the iPod on top, and scooted awkwardly from the bed. "Who—?"

"He didn't offer his name He just asked me to fetch you. Older guy, bald on top."

Dad. Scottlyn's stomach fell into her socks. *What's he doing here? Maybe he's changed his mind.* She swallowed back the hurt and anger of their final fight, but she refused to give in to hope. She knew her father well enough to know he wouldn't change his mind. "Thanks. Will you tell him I'll be down in a couple of minutes?"

"Take your time. He didn't look to be in a hurry. Just fixed himself a cup of coffee and took a seat. I'll tell him you're on the way."

Scottlyn held her smile until the door closed. Then she rushed to her dresser, ran a brush through her hair, and glossed her lips. Her hands shook as she smoothed her shirt and turned and twisted in front of the mirror. There was no way to guess what he wanted, but she wasn't about to go downstairs looking less than her best. She wouldn't give him the satisfaction of thinking that she was unhappy with her choices or pining for home.

A few minutes later, she entered the dining room and stood just inside the door. Her dad met her eyes from across the room, his gaze never leaving her face. *He still refuses to acknowledge you, Mercie. Like ignoring you will make you go away.* Scottlyn squared her shoulders and returned his scrutiny. Silence stretched between them. It had been a month since he'd ordered her out of his house.

He leaned back in his seat and motioned to the empty chairs around the table. "Sit down."

His confrontational tone sent a wave of nerves skittering up Scottlyn's spine. Why couldn't he just be a dad? She'd never needed—or longed for—a mother more. She slipped into the chair farthest from him, leaned back, and crossed her arms over her belly. She didn't speak but simply raised her eyebrows in invitation.

"Still rebellious and insolent, I see. I'd hoped a few weeks on your own would've adjusted your attitude. I can see I was wrong." They stared silently at each other for several seconds, the only noise that of their breathing. "Have you nothing to say for yourself?"

Scottlyn shrugged. *Don't cry... Don't cry... Don't cry.* "Does is matter what I have to say? Have you changed your mind? Have you decided to acknowledge your grandchild? Cause if you have, I'd love to come back home—"

"Never!" The word rang through the room like a death knell. Her father jumped to his feet, face purple with rage, blood veins pulsing along the sides of his neck. The jacket he'd hung on the back of the chair began to slip to the floor. He grabbed it and threw it on the table, barely missing his half empty cup. "You'll not bring that...that...misbegotten child into my home." His chest heaved with a few ragged breaths before he continued. "I've had all of this nonsense from you I intend to take, young lady. I've offered you every logical solution, and still you choose to defy me by ruining your life." He paced away from the table and prowled the back of the room. "You're putting me in a difficult situation, and I resent it."

Scottlyn lowered her gaze to her swollen abdomen and then looked back at her father. "What difficult position are *you* in?"

"Don't sass me."

She raised her hands. "Dad, you raised me to be obedient and respectful. I'm not trying to make you crazy, but can't you please...just for one minute...try to see this from my side of the fence? It's not just my life at stake here—"

"Bah!" Her father cut her off with a flip of his hand. "You don't know anything about life. How are you going to make a home for yourself and a baby? You can't...you won't." He reclaimed his seat and studied her from across the table. "I've done all I can to bring you to your senses. Now we'll let the courts handle it. You're still a minor,

Scottlyn. You have no home, no means of support, nothing to give a child except poverty and grief."

It was Scottlyn's turn to stand. "That's not true! I love her. Why can't you see that?"

"Love is a poor commodity when your belly is empty."

Scottlyn rubbed her face with her hands. She looked at the man she'd lived with her whole life and saw a stranger. "You are such a sad, cold man." She waved to the door. "Just get out and leave me alone."

He rose slowly, rested his hands on the table, and leaned forward. "Scottlyn Denise Rich. You will not use that tone of voice with me. I've never raised a hand to you in anger, but—"

"And you aren't about to start now." The same housemother who'd fetched her from upstairs earlier stepped into the room and put an arm around Scottlyn's shoulders. "Please, allow me to show you to our front door. You will do us all a favor by not returning."

Her father sputtered, face turning an even deeper shade of purple. Scottlyn knew that face well enough to know the explosion behind it. But instead of that, he snatched up his jacket, accidentally sending the Styrofoam cup rolling across the table and onto the floor. The spilled coffee spread over the wooden surface in a brown puddle. Her father pointed. "You see that? That's your life, Scottlyn. A big nasty mess, getting bigger and bigger, as long as no one takes any action to put a stop to it." He stomped to the doorway, turned, and faced her. "Thirty days. That's the time you have left to get this whole thing out of your system. Four weeks from today, you'll be getting a summons to appear before a judge in family court to put an end to this, once and for all."

"I hate you!" Scottlyn shrugged off the housemother's arm and raced up the stairs as fast as her five month pregnancy would allow. She slammed her door with a satisfying bang. She was sorely tempted to open it and slam it a second time. Inside the room, she leaned against the door, swiped at the tears on her cheeks, and forced her breathing to return to normal. She crossed to the bed and lay down in the abandoned nest of pillows. As Scottlyn grew quiet, the baby began to squirm.

Mercie's kicks and jabs made her smile through her tears. She picked up the iPod, turned on the music, and pressed the ear buds to her abdomen. "Here you go, baby. Don't worry, everything's going to be fine. I'm your mommy, and nothing will ever change that." The baby settled, and Scottlyn drew in a deep breath. Her father's words came back to haunt her. *You have no home, no means of support, nothing to give a child except poverty and grief.* She hugged her arms around her middle and turned her face into the pillows. Thirty days? *What am I supposed to do?*

CHAPTER SEVEN

"Dr. Moore's office."

Diana pitched her voice a little louder than normal in order to be heard above the sounds of crying children. "Lynette, it's Diana. Have you got a minute?

"Sure. Hang on for a sec, OK?"

Diana heard muffled voices and a few clicks followed by several seconds of silence before her friend came back on the line.

"I'm here. I had to transfer your call to the back hall. It's shot day and there isn't a dry eye in the house. What's up?"

"Nothing major. Do you mind if we have dinner at six thirty tonight instead of five."

"You got a date?"

Diana laughed. "Hardly. Something's wrong with Scottlyn. Her eyes have been red all day, and she was listless and unresponsive in class. I've only known her a week, but this is not like her. Poor kid doesn't have much of a support system. I told her to wait for me outside the teacher's lounge after school, and I'd take her home. I need to find out what's wrong."

"I'm proud of you."

"Why?"

"You've really taken an interest in this girl. I think you're good for each other."

"Yeah, well, that remains to be seen. Dinner at six thirty?"

"That's fine. I'll say a prayer for both of you in the meantime."

Diana slid the phone into her bag and headed to the teacher's lounge. She found Scottlyn waiting for her on the hard bench, head resting on the raised back, eyes closed.

"Hey, I'm ready if you are."

Scottlyn's eyes jerked open as she scrambled to her feet. "Sorry. I didn't get much sleep last night."

"Baby keep you awake?"

The youngster shrugged. "Not the baby. Just...stuff."

Diana let the subject drop until they got to her car. The February weather had taken a springtime turn. No wind and almost seventy degrees. *Milkshake weather.* She marveled at the thought. The weather wasn't the only thing changing. Her appetite seemed to be coming back in a big way.

She scooted behind the wheel of the Camry and buckled her seat belt, waiting for Scottlyn to do the same. "You girls hungry?"

Scottlyn chuckled. "We are always hungry." She jerked. "Ouch! Brattling!"

"You OK?"

"This kid has a vicious kick. Give me your hand."

Diana allowed Scottlyn to take her hand and place it on her stomach. Several seconds passed. "What am I supposed to be feeling?"

"Wait for it."

When the sharp little kick came, it was hard enough to raise Diana's eyebrows. She left her hand in place and waited for a repeat performance. The second jab was just as hard. "Does she do that all day?"

Scottlyn shook her head, grinning down at her belly. "No. As long as I'm moving, she's pretty quiet. The motion must keep her pacified. The minute I sit or lie down, her work out begins."

"You're going to have your hands more than full in a few months." Diana's casual remark must have hit a tender target. Her heart broke when Scottlyn's blue eyes filled with tears.

"Yeah, well not if my dad has anything to say about it." She sniffed and searched her purse. "Sorry. I think I've got a tissue in here someplace."

Diana leaned across the seat, opened the glove box, and pulled out a small package. "Here you go. Don't apologize. I knew something was up with you today. Do you want to talk about it?"

Scottlyn shrugged and dabbed at her eyes. "I don't know what good talking will do." She sniffed again and stared out the windshield. "It's just all so hard."

"Scottlyn, let me help if I can."

"Dad came by the shelter last night. He's still so angry that I won't let him dictate my life. Now he's threatened to take me to court."

"For what?"

"Family court. He says they can force me to give my baby up because I have nothing to offer her. And I really don't, not material things, anyway. But I love her." Scottlyn sniffed and dabbed at her eyes. "Doesn't that count for something?" She pulled a second tissue free and blew her nose. "If he'd just leave me alone... If everyone would let me be... I just want to be the mother to Mercie that I never had. Why is that so hard for everyone to understand?"

Diana sat in silence for a few seconds, searching for words and direction. *Father, this is the saddest thing I've ever seen in my life.* The voice in her heart was insistent.

Share hope with her.

Diana shook her head. Hope? Do I really have that to share?

"Sweetheart, dry your face and look at me." She waited until she was sure she had Scottlyn's attention. "Let's deal with your father's threats first. I'll help you find a lawyer to talk to if you like, but I think he's blowing smoke. You have a roof over your head and the baby's. You aren't into drugs or anything, so they can't claim that you're unfit to keep your child. No court is going to take your baby away from you just because it's what he wants."

"Really?"

"I'm a teacher not a lawyer, but my husband and I dealt with our share of them when we were trying to adopt a child of our own." She placed her hand back on Scottlyn's stomach. "This baby is yours, and as long as you continue to make good decisions, you're they only one with any say about how she's raised."

A sigh of relief shuddered through Scottlyn's chest. "I worried all last night, trying to figure out what I was going to do. It's nice to have someone on my side for a change."

Share hope with her.

Diana glanced up at the roof of the car and sighed. *All right.*

"I think you have more people on your side than you realize. God puts each of us on this earth for a reason. He brings people into our lives just when we need them."

Scottlyn tilted her head and studied Diana. "Do you really think so?"

"I know so. The Bible says He knows each of us before we're ever formed. Not only does He know us, he has a plan for us. You, me...and Mercie."

Scottlyn circled her hands over the baby in her womb with a frown. "God wanted me to be raped?"

"No honey. We all make choices. The boy who raped you made a terrible and selfish choice. But you...you've made the most unselfish choices I've ever heard of. I think God is directing those choices. I think, if you'll listen, He'll continue to do so."

"Do you really believe that?"

"I really do."

Scottlyn stared out the window for a few seconds. "That's sort of neat when you think about it. It makes my heart feel funny though, sort of light and happy, like I need to know more."

Well, that was easy. "Do you have a Bible?"

"They have some in the library at the shelter."

"Great. I have an extra homework assignment for you this week. I want you to read the book of John. Take the time to go through it thoroughly. Catch up with me after class if you have questions about what you're reading."

Scottlyn nodded. "I can do that. Anything else?"

"Would you like to go to church with me next Sunday?"

Her student shrank down in the car seat. "Ah, gee, I don't know. Can I give you a yes on the Bible thing and a maybe on the invitation? I promise I'll think about it."

Diana nodded and started the car. "That works. Now, let's go spoil our dinners."

CHAPTER EIGHT

Lynette was halfway through a basket of chips by the time Diana arrived at the restaurant. She slid into the seat across from her friend and helped herself to a handful of the crispy triangles. She filled Lynette in on her conversation with Scottlyn while they waited for the waitress to come and take their orders.

"That poor child was terrified that they could force her to give up her baby. I haven't met her father, but I'd like to ring his neck."

"You did the right thing. If he keeps bothering her, she can petition the court for emancipation. There are social programs available to her as well. They sure won't give her an extravagant lifestyle, but she can receive enough to keep body and soul together until she finishes school and finds a job."

Diana crossed her arms and sat back. "It's so sad. She's done everything right, and she keeps getting slapped down for it. I mean, how much is one young girl supposed to take before she cracks? I did get to witness to her a bit before I took her home, though. She promised to read John this week. I hope that will spark a desire to learn more."

"You really like this girl, don't you?"

Diana started to answer, but the young waitress approached their table. "Sorry for the wait, ladies. You two are later than normal, and we're swamped. Do you know what you want?"

Diana nodded. "I want two chicken enchiladas, rice, and beans." She tipped the basket and peered inside. "Gonna need some more chips, too, and could you bring out some flour tortillas when you come back?"

"Got it." She turned to Lynette. "And for you?"

Lynette decided on a half order of shrimp fajitas. The waitress departed for the kitchen and Lynette frowned at Diana. "Who are you, and what have you done with my friend?"

"What?"

"Diana, you ordered a complete meal, and I didn't have to bribe or threaten you first. What gives?"

She shrugged. "Just getting my appetite back, I guess. You want to be really shocked?"

Lynette nodded.

"I had a milkshake an hour ago."

Her friend stared, obviously speechless.

"It's weird. I've eaten three full meals a day, all week. Now I'm snacking. That's not all. I've had some really interesting conversations with God this week, too."

"About?"

"You wouldn't believe it if I told you."

Their food arrived, and they were silent as the waitress distributed the hot dishes. Lynette offered a quick grace, and they both dove into their food.

Lynette rolled fragrant shrimp and peppers into a tortilla and sprinkled it with grated cheese. "Keep talking girlfriend. What have you and the Man Upstairs been discussing?"

Diana cut one of her enchiladas into bite sized pieces. *She's going to think I've lost my mind.* Finally she shrugged and leaned forward. "You know Chuck's Rav4?"

Lynette chewed, her face wrinkled in concentration. She swallowed. "You mean the one in your garage that you haven't touched in almost a year and a half? Yeah, I know the one. What about it?"

"I think God wants me to give it to Scottlyn."

"OK... And you think that why?"

Diana told her about Scottlyn's wish wall and her surprise at seeing Chuck's vehicle among the pictures. "I didn't say anything to her. I still haven't said anything, but it's just sitting there, paid for, taking up space. I've tried to put the thought out of my mind. I mean, who goes around handing out cars to people? But I can't get past it."

"Wow. That's...amazing."

"There's more."

She continued when Lynette simply raised an eyebrow. "Did you hear Jeremy's testimony yesterday morning?"

Lynette nodded. "Wasn't that wonderful? I still get tears in my eyes when I think about it."

"What if I told you that I think God wants me to *entertain* Scottlyn?"

"Entertain how?"

"You know the verse Jeremy read about entertaining angels? Like making a place for them in your home? I think that's what God's asking me to do for Scottlyn. It goes along with the other verse Jeremy read. The one about seeing someone in need and just saying, 'good luck,' or, 'things will work out,' instead of using your resources to meet that need. I have the resources to meet a lot of Scottlyn's needs. It's my choice how to use them."

Lynette chewed and motioned for Diana to get back to her dinner. They ate in silence for a few minutes. Diana wasn't quite sure what to do now that she'd put God's prodding into words. Lynette was obviously working to take in everything she'd heard.

Lynette's fork clattered into her empty plate. "I think you should do it."

"Really? You don't think I'm nuts for thinking about opening my home to a person I've only known for a week?"

She waved Diana's words away. "Honey, when God tells you to do something, you're on His time, not yours." Lynette scooted her plate away and leaned forward on folded arms. "I want you to consider a few things." She nodded at Diana's empty plate. "You cleaned your plate, just like last week while we were having our first conversation about Scottlyn."

Diana thought back and nodded. "I've been sleeping better too."

"Here's what I think. Scottyln's situation has taken your mind off your grief. You've got something new to focus on, so you aren't thinking about Chuck twenty-four hours a day."

Diana's eyes filled with tears. "I don't want to leave him behind."

"Oh honey, you're not leaving *him*, but you are leaving the grief. That's a good thing. Answer a question for me. Other than Chuck's death, what's the one thing you regret most about your life?"

Diana's answer was immediate. "Not being able to have a family. Not having someone to lavish my time and attention on..."

Lynette grinned as Diana's statement trailed off. "The lights just came on, didn't they?"

"Do you think?"

"I think you have a child looking for a home and someone to love her. I think there's a baby on the way who's gonna need a grandma to spoil her. I think God's trying to fill up your empty house with all the dreams you thought were long gone." She reached across and took Diana's hand. "I think if you don't do what God's urging you to do, you're going to look back on this moment and regret it for the rest of your life."

CHAPTER NINE

Diana stood in the doorway of one of four bedrooms. She and Chuck had fallen in love with this house because it was big enough to raise the family they'd hoped to have. This room and the one next to it, connected by a full bath, were her favorites. Perfect for two little girls or two little boys. *Even more perfect for a young girl and her baby.* "God, you never cease to amaze me."

Over the years, their hopes for a family died. The rooms became Chuck's home office and her craft room. She'd been in neither since his death, too heart sick to deal with Chuck's personal items, too despondent to indulge in the hobbies she loved.

She walked through the rooms now, studying furnishings and fixtures with a critical eye. She spoke to the walls and hoped that maybe, just maybe, Chuck could hear.

"I remember when you decided to turn this room into an office. I cried. How could you give up on our dreams so easily? You laughed while you held me and told me that if God answered our prayers for a family, you could change it back, but there wasn't any reason to let the space go to waste in the meantime." She moved through the connecting bath and into her abandoned craft room.

"A few years later when I moved some of my stuff in here, you stood in the door and teased me." She ran her hand along the bookcases Chuck had built for her one year. Her fingers came away coated in months' worth of dust. "We had some good times here, made some great memories. You, clicking away on your computer, me grading papers or working on whatever caught my fancy at the moment. Right here, next to each other, talking back and forth through the open doors. All we had was each other and, in the end, that was all we needed." Diana lifted a picture off the shelf, smiling into Chuck's brown eyes. "We were going to spend forever together. How come forever came so soon?" She tapped a finger on his cleft chin. "I miss you so much."

She replaced the picture and turned back to the room with a determined sigh. "I need boxes and paint. The carpets need to be cleaned, and I need bedroom and nursery furniture." Her shoulders slumped. "I need help."

Diana dug her phone out of her pocket. She dialed Lynette's number and barely waited for her friend to speak. "I'm gonna do it and you're gonna help."

"Yay! What do you want me to do?"

"Keep your evenings free for the next few days. There is so much to do. These rooms need to be stripped down to the carpet and bare walls. I'm calling Millicent in on this, too. She has access to Scottlyn's wish wall, and I need copies of those pictures."

"What are you thinking?"

Diana laughed. "Well, I always envisioned a canopy bed and white furniture trimmed in gold—"

"Oh my."

"But Scottlyn's a little old for the Disney Princess look."

"Whew!"

"Yes, Lynette, I do have a brain. Can you meet me at the hardware store after work tomorrow? We can rent a carpet shampooer and look at paint samples. I'm thinking pink for the baby's room, but maybe a soft mauve with cream trim for Scottlyn's room."

"Ohh...I like the mauve, but we're going to have to talk about the pink. Why don't I come back to your house once we're done, and I'll help you start boxing stuff up?"

Diana swallowed back the sudden tears clogging her throat. *Father, I know I'm doing the right thing. Please give me the strength and peace I need to get it done.*

"Diana...?"

Diana forced herself beyond the moment and found excitement replacing her melancholy. "Deal. I'll make us some sandwiches, and we can eat while we work. If we can get things cleaned out and the painting done, maybe we can go into the city on Saturday and look for furniture."

~ * ~

The next four days passed in a blur of activity. Under Lynette's gentle exterior lurked a slave driver. She pressed forward every evening with *just one more box* or *just one more wall.* Occasionally, an item or action sparked a painful memory that threatened to wrap Diana back in her blanket of grief. Lynette became an unending source of support and comfort. Each night, Diana fell into bed, bone tired, and rose to function on autopilot the following day.

Scottlyn came to class each day and sat with Diana during lunch to discuss the chapters she'd read the night before, not only John but most of the four gospels. Church on Sunday was still a maybe, but the girl had promised to call her by Saturday night to let her know one way or the other.

The work on the house progressed, and each time Diana and Scottlyn talked, Diana found herself biting her lip to keep from spoiling the surprise. Scottlyn seemed to be at peace for the moment and in the end, Diana found she just couldn't surrender the moment of surprise she envisioned on her student's face.

She pulled off the last piece of masking tape and backed out of the newly painted nursery on Friday night, almost tripping over Lynette in the process. "Sorry."

"No prob." Lynette put an arm around Diana's shoulders, and they surveyed the fruits of their labor. "It looks really great."

"Yep. I like the yellow you talked me into. It's cheerful. And the Mary-had-a-little-lamb border that Millicent recommended when she gave us the pictures of Scottlyn's wish wall looks great. I don't know how she got that piece of info out of Scottlyn without giving away the surprise, but it's the perfect finishing touch."

Lynette nodded. "Let's get this door back on the hinges, and we're done."

"Oh, thank goodness!" Diana stretched and arched her back, grinning when it popped loudly. "I'm too old for this. I didn't really think we could get everything done in four nights."

"Are we still on for furniture tomorrow?" Lynette asked.

"That's the fun part. Want to meet for breakfast first?"

They maneuvered the door into place. "Hold it right there." Lynette reached for the hammer and the door pins. Three taps of the hammer, and their project was complete. "Breakfast sounds great. Right now, all I want is something cold to drink and a chair to collapse in."

Diana swiped at the newly hung door with a dust rag. "I can fix that for you. Come on into the kitchen."

Lynette popped the top on the frosty diet cola. "How was our little mother today?"

Diana rummaged in the cabinet for a bag of chips to go with their drinks before she fell into her own chair. "Full of questions. Why didn't Jesus just tell them flat out who he was? How come he used so many stories? And the biggie for her, how could Jesus love Judas and forgive him after what he did?"

Lynette munched on a chip and nodded. "Poor baby. She's dealt with so much betrayal in her own life, It doesn't surprise me that forgiveness is an issue for her." She stopped when Diana's phone rang.

Diana glanced at the clock. *Eleven o'clock...who in the world...?* "Hello?"

"Mrs. Kensington?"

"Scottlyn? Are you crying? What's wrong?"

The youngster on the other end of the phone gulped for breath. "I'm fine. I'm better than fine. I know I shouldn't have called so late, but I had to tell someone or burst. I just finished reading John for the second time and I...I asked Jesus to help me understand, and He did! I get it now."

Diana listened with tears streaming down her own face.

Lynette leaned forward. "Is it the baby?" she whispered.

Diana shook her head and placed a finger across her lips. She quietly placed the phone on speaker and placed it in the center of the table.

Scottlyn continued. "I didn't know it would feel like this. I didn't know anything could feel like this. If it weren't for Mercie, I'd climb up on the roof and shout it to the world. Jesus loves me! Me! And He loves my baby, and it really is going to be all right. I still don't know how, but I know it." She paused, but her ragged breathing echoed through the phone. "So I needed to tell you, and I wanted to accept your invitation to church on Sunday."

Diana retrieved the phone. "Scottlyn, I'm so proud of you. It *is* going to be OK. I'll pick you up at nine thirty. Now, go get some sleep...and stay off the roof."

Scottlyn hung up, and Diana stared at the phone for several seconds. "Well, what do you think about that?"

"I think God has a plan, and we finished those rooms just in time." She raised her soda can in a toast, and Diana clinked hers against it. Then, in the way of women when there are no words to express their emotions, they collapsed into each other's arms and ended their day's labor with a good cry.

CHAPTER TEN

Sunday morning, Scottlyn's breath fogged around her, and she pulled her jacket tighter while she paced the sidewalk to keep warm. The jacket didn't quite come together around her middle. She heard a motor in the distance and watched the road for Mrs. Kensington.

A red vehicle turned the corner, coming in her direction. Scottlyn dismissed it and continued to pace. Mrs. Kensington drove a silver Camry.

The red Rav4 stopped at the curb. The windows were darkly tinted, and Scottlyn couldn't see who was behind the wheel. Probably a visitor for one of the other girls. *I'm gonna have one of those someday.* She rubbed her gloved hands over her belly. "See that Mercie? Just like the one on our wish wall."

The door of the SUV opened, and Mrs. Kensington climbed out. "Are you ready?"

"Oh, wow...yeah. I was looking for your car. I didn't know you had one of these, too."

"It belonged to my husband."

"Cool. I love these things." She reached for the passenger side door.

"Hold up. You have a driver's license, right?"

"Yeah."

Her teacher crossed in front of the idling vehicle. "Why don't you drive, then? I saw one like this on your wall the other day. If you're hoping to own one down the road, you should see if you really like it."

"Seriously?"

Mrs. Kensington opened the passenger door and scooted inside. "Absolutely. Take us to church. I'll navigate."

"Frosty cool!"

~ * ~

Diana stayed nearby and watched Scottlyn closely throughout the morning. She needn't have worried. Several kids from Eden Heights attended service with Diana. Scottlyn found the same acceptance here that she'd found at school.

The youngster dove into the worship service with a freedom few adults could have managed. She might not know the words to the songs, but she followed them on the projection screen, clapping with the congregation and bouncing in time to the music.

When they sat for the morning sermon, Scottlyn leaned over to whisper in her ear. "You guys sing like this all the time?"

Diana nodded.

"I like it!"

Scottlyn focused her attention on the minister, but Diana found her mind drifting to what came next. *Have I done the right thing? I'm taking an awful lot for granted. What if this isn't what she wants? What do I really know about this girl and her situation? Have I lost my mind?* Questions and doubts. *Chuck, I wish you were here. We could do this so much better together.*

Follow the plan, daughter.

Diana chuckled at the words. *What plan?* If anything in

her life had ever been done with less of a plan, she'd be hard pressed to point it out. The congregation stood for the dismissal prayer. She turned to face Scottlyn as people milled around them.

"How did you like it?"

"It was...interesting." She looked around the sanctuary. "I haven't been to church much, so this is sort of new. Can I come to service with you again tonight?"

"Absolutely." Diana took a deep breath. *Here goes nothing.* "In fact. If you're free for the afternoon, I've got some things I'd like to show you at my house."

Scottlyn shrugged. "Sure. I don't have anywhere else to be."

Diana tossed her the keys. "You're driving."

"Thanks!"

Fifteen minutes later, Scottlyn came to a cautious stop in Diana's driveway. She turned off the engine and stared at the house through the windshield.

"This place is huge."

Diana followed her gaze and tried to see it though fresh eyes. "Well, not as big as the shelter by any means, but I have plenty of room." She motioned to the interior of the Rav4. "So, what did you think of your test drive? Still think it's your dream vehicle."

"It's a terrific set of wheels, for sure. Thanks for letting me play with it." She removed the keys from the ignition and offered them to Diana. "Here you go."

"Keep them."

Scottlyn's eyes grew big. "You're going to let me drive it again tonight? Wow!"

Diana shook her head. "Tonight and for as long as you want."

"Umm...I...do what?"

"Scottlyn, my husband died..." Diana's throat clogged

on the words. She pushed back the tears and swallowed the obstruction. "My husband Chuck died last year. This was his. It's paid for. Today is the first day it's been out of the garage since...since he drove it last. I want you to have it."

Scottlyn bowed her head over the steering wheel. "I don't even know what to say. I don't want to sound ungrateful, but I can't accept this."

Diana's heart tumbled into her shoes. *I knew this was a harebrained idea.*

The youngster continued. "I mean, I don't have a job, so I can't afford the insurance or the gas." She ran her hands over the dash. Diana could see the desire in her eyes. "If there were any way I could say yes, I would. I'd kiss your feet for a gift like this and be your slave for life, but you should keep it." She held out the keys.

Diana reached out to close Scottlyn's fingers around the keys. "You don't understand. The gas and insurance are on me for as long as you're in school. I knew when I saw the picture on your wish wall that God wanted you to have it, and Chuck would agree."

Scottlyn looked from their joined hands into Diana's face. She lifted a shoulder as her face crumpled. "Why? Why would you do this for me?"

Diana hugged her over the console. "There's more. Would you like to see?"

Scottlyn sat up, swiped her face with the sleeve of her jacket, and nodded. "It can't possibly be as good as this, but I'm game."

They entered the house through the garage. Diana led her straight to the nursery. She leaned against the closed door and met Scottlyn's eyes. There should be words at a time like this, but her throat had gone as dry as the Sahara. She licked her lips, opened the door, and allowed

Scottlyn to precede her into the room.

Her student took one step across the threshold and froze. She turned her head and looked at Diana over her shoulder. "What did you do?"

"Do you like it?"

Scottlyn moved forward in slow motion. Her fingertips brushed the top of the oak chest of drawers and moved to the matching changing table. She came to a stop beside the crib and stroked the smooth wood of the slatted front panel. The rocker in the corner completed the ensemble. Her breath shuddered in her chest. "It's Mercie's wish room." She turned and faced Diana. "I don't understand."

Diana took her hand. "I didn't understand a week ago myself. Come with me, there's one more thing to see." She led the way through the connecting bath and into the second bedroom. Here, a double bed dominated the space. The chest, dresser, and nightstand all matched the oak furniture in the other room.

Scottlyn turned in a slow circle. When she stopped in front of Diana, her eyes were damp but steady, her voice calm. "If I had a wish room of my own, this would be it."

Diana broke her gaze to look around the room. "Chuck and I always hoped to fill these rooms with children of our own. It took us a long time to accept the fact that God had a different plan for us. It's taken even longer for me to find that plan on my own."

Her eyes went back to Scottlyn's face. The hope she saw there almost broke her heart. "We haven't had a chance to get to know each other as well as I'd like, but I know that you're a young lady of principles, courage, and compassion. You've made decisions that adversely affected your life in order to guarantee a future for your daughter. I admire that more than I can say.

"I'd love to offer you and Mercie a home for as long as you need one. It doesn't have a white picket fence, and we'll have to discuss the puppy when the time comes, but if you're interested, we'll take that Rav4 over to the shelter, pick up your stuff, and get you moved in this afternoon."

Scottlyn hugged her arms around herself. "Mrs. Kensington—"

"If we're gonna be house mates, let's make it Diana, at least when we aren't in class."

She nodded. "Diana...I'd like that, more than you can know. I'm still not sure why you're doing all of this."

Diana put an arm around Scottlyn's shoulder. "The whys aren't important. We'll have lots of time to figure it out. All that's really important is working together and following God's plan—for Mercie's sake.

EPILOGUE

Scottlyn's eyes jerked open. She lay still for a few seconds, listening for whatever it was that had yanked her out of a rare night of sound sleep. *Nothing.*

She shifted in the bed in search of a cooler spot between the sheets. The last few months had given her a whole new appreciation for the old term *a bun in the oven.* She was hot all of the time. Oklahoma's late spring humidity didn't help.

Scottlyn lowered her lids and allowed her mind to drift. Maybe she could slide back into that peaceful place.

A tiny piece of anatomy jammed into her left kidney. "Oww..." She rubbed her swollen belly. "Calm down, Mercie, you're killing me!" The baby squirmed under her hands. "You're just as anxious as I am, aren't you? I can't wait to see you in person, but unless we're hatching tonight..." Scottlyn's eyes went wide as water...*I hope it's water...* gushed onto the sheets. She whipped the cover back and scrambled to the her feet as fast as her forty-one week pregnancy would allow. Her nightgown clung to her legs, chilling the flesh that had been overheated just moments before.

She picked at the fabric, trying to hold it away from her, afraid to move. "Diana!" Scottlyn's breath went jerky, and everything she'd learned in her childbirth classes evaporated from her brain. *What do I do...what do I do?*

"Diana!"

The hall door swung open. "What in the world...?" the older woman hurried across the room. "Is it time?"

"I think my water broke."

Diana glanced at the bed. "I think you're right. Contractions?"

Scottlyn shook her head.

"Let's get you to the hospital."

"I need a shower." She looked down at her sodden gown. "Yucky doesn't even begin to cover what this is. Do you think there's time?"

Diana chewed her lip. "I have as much experience with this as you do...which is zip...but they say first babies are notoriously slow, so go for it. I'll get myself ready." She glanced around the room. "Your bag is in the car. Do you need me to take anything else out?"

Scottlyn shuffled to her chest of drawers and rummaged. She nodded to the chair in the corner. "Body pillow and iPod." Her hands stilled and she bowed her head.

"Scottlyn?"

She turned with a fresh change of clothes in her hands. "Diana, I'm so scared."

"You'll do fine," Diana said.

Scottlyn looked down at her belly. "Not about this. I'm more than ready to have my body back." She met Diana's gaze. "I'm sixteen. What if I don't...what if I...?" Her frustrated sigh echoed. "How can I be a good mother when I never had one?"

Diana put an arm around Scottlyn's shoulders and squeezed. "I repeat, you'll do fine." She rested her other hand on the mount of belly. "Miss Mercie is going to come into this world loved and cared for. I think the rest will come with time. Now go get that shower before

Mercie gets impatient to meet her mommy."

"Thanks, Diana. Remind me later."

"Of what?"

"I've got a feeling it's going to be a long night. Don't let me forget how very blessed I am."

Scottlyn waddled into the bathroom that separated her bedroom from the nursery. She striped out of the wet gown and adjusted the water. She glanced through the connecting door and tried to imagine herself there with a baby. The sheer magnitude of that responsibility accelerated her breathing. *I can do this...I can do this...Jesus, with Your help every single day, I can do this."*

The prayer calmed her nerves. She showered and lathered up her hair. Shampoo bubbles were swirling down the drain when the first contraction nearly doubled her over. Scottlyn braced a hand against the wall and breathed through the pain. When the band around her middle loosened, she straightened. "Whew...that was...extreme."

She rushed through the rest of her shower, dressed, dried her hair, and took the time to apply blush and mascara, pausing for two more contractions along the way.

Diana looked up when Scottlyn entered the living room and shook her head. "Good grief. You're on your way to give birth, not attend the prom."

Scottlyn tossed her long blonde hair over her shoulder. "There's no reason why I can't look good. Besides, I don't want Mercie to think she has a hag for a mother." She stopped on an indrawn breath.

"Contraction?"

She nodded and waited for it to pass. "That makes four so far, eight to ten minutes apart."

Diana grabbed her keys. "Then let's get this show on

the road."

~ * ~

While the nurses prepped Scottlyn for the birth of her daughter, Diana paced the hallway outside the door. Life as she knew it was about to change in a major way. It made her nervous, it excited her, and, though she'd never admit it to Scottlyn, she was terrified.

The swinging door flew open, and a nurse hurried out and away.

"Can I go in now?" Diana called after her.

The nurse took a couple of steps back. "You're her labor coach, right?"

Diana nodded.

"Then that's an excellent idea. I'm on my way to call the doctor. We're about to have a baby."

She turned to leave, but Diana grabbed her arm. "Wait...what? We just got here."

"Yep. That baby is a week overdue and anxious to greet the world. Better get in there. I think Mom could really use a hand to hold about now." She hurried away.

Diana's feet rooted themselves to the floor.

"Diana!"

The single frantic word loosened her feet and sent her sailing through the door.

~ * ~

The contraction started at her toes, worked its way passed her knees, and squeezed her midsection in a two-ton vice. Scottlyn transferred that pain to Diana's hand.

"Scottlyn, breathe."

"I can't." The words were a whispered groan.

"Yes, you can." Diana leaned over the bed. "Look at me."

Scottlyn's eyes focused on Diana's face. Her surrogate mother panted in short bursts. Scottlyn did her best to mimic her and went limp as the pain released its grip.

"I need some drugs."

"Two late for that, sweetheart. Keep your eye on the prize. Women have been doing this since time began."

The next contraction came fast and hot. Scottlyn closed her eyes. "I'm not a woman, I'm a kid."

"You're about to be a mother. Breathe!"

Socttlyn's eye's jerked open. "I need to push!"

"No, you don't," the nurse told her. "I know it's a hard sensation to resist, but you aren't ready yet. Breathe for us."

"I hate that word." But she took the short breaths. Once the pain subsided she looked at the nurse. "Where is Dr. Mason?"

"She's—"

A short, gray-haired woman wearing pink scrubs pushed into the room. She took in the situation at a glance and crossed to the bed. "In a hurry, are we?"

Scottlyn nodded. "Someone is."

Dr. Mason patted Scottlyn's leg. "Let's take a look." She lifted the sheet, and her eyebrows rose. "Are you ready?"

"More than," Scottlyn assured her.

"Then let's have a baby."

The room exploded into a frenzy of action. Scottlyn couldn't keep up as the next pain took her.

"Breath through this one," Dr. Mason said. "Then take a few seconds to regroup. We're going to push with the next contraction. I'd say baby in thirty minutes or so."

Scottlyn lay back in the bed and looked at the ceiling,

trying to gather her strength.

Diana brushed hair out of her face. "You're doing great."

"It's not supposed to happen this fast."

"I don't think Mercie read the rule book." She glanced at the monitor. "Get ready."

Dr. Mason took her position. "Okay, Scottlyn, I want you to give me three good pushes during this contraction. Diana, when I tell you, I want you count to ten. Scottlyn, you push as long as she's counting. And...now."

"One, two, three..."

Scottlyn tucked her chin to her chest and pushed for all she was worth.

"Hold it." The doctor told her. "Oh, this little lady has places to be. Nurse give me a suction bulb. Scottlyn, did you order blonde curly hair?"

"Is she here?"

The doctor shook her head. "One more push should do it, though. On my mark. Ready...go."

Scottlyn bore down and fell back into the pillows as the pressure and pain gave way to an overwhelming sense of release. She smiled as the room echoed with outraged crying.

Diana leaned close. "You did it!"

"I need to see her."

"Thirty seconds. We're cutting the cord." The doctor monologued the procedure. "And here you go."

Scottlyn's eyes filled as they laid the baby on her stomach. She reached down tentatively and stroked the fine curls. "Diana?"

"She's a beauty, and from where I stand, I can count ten fingers and ten toes."

A nurse leaned over and smiled at Scottlyn. "I'm going to borrow her for just a minute, then you two can get better acquainted." She lifted the baby away, and Scottlyn followed her every move with a fierce possessiveness she'd never experienced before.

She watched as they took Mercie's temperature, put drops in her eyes, and gave her a quick rub down. Another member of the team attached a plastic bracelet around her ankle. The nurse lifted her again and brought her back to the bed. "This one's a keeper, seven pounds, eight ounces, and eighteen inches long." She shifted Scottlyn's gown and laid the baby on the bare skin of her chest.

"This is called skin to skin time," she whispered as she brought the sheet back up to cover Scottlyn and the baby. "There are some studies that show that babies who get a bit of early bonding time sleep better and seem to be a little calmer."

Mercie squirmed for a few seconds and then stilled as her heart beat against her mother's. Scottlyn ran a finger down the soft cheek, while the baby's rosebud mouth made tiny sucking motions. Scottlyn looked up at the nurse. "Is she hungry?"

"They almost always are," the nurse answered with a grin. "But she seems pretty content for now. She'll let us know when that changes."

Scottlyn nodded, glanced around, and found Diana still standing beside the bed. "I'm a mom." Emotion clogged her throat. "Thank you."

Tears glinted in Diana's eyes. "You did all the work." She stroked a finger around Mercie's ear. "She's beautiful and perfect. Thank you for allowing me to be a part of the process."

The doctor cleared her throat from the foot of the bed. "Well, you've certainly livened up my morning. But then the only hard and fast rule about delivering babies is that there are no hard and fast rules. Each time is unique. I do have one suggestion for your next pregnancy."

Scottlyn raised her eyebrows.

"You need to get to the hospital way before the first contraction." She chuckled and nodded toward Scottlyn and Diana. "Well done, both of you."

The next couple of hours disappeared in a flurry of activity as Scottlyn fed Mercie, moved to a new room, wolfed down a predawn snack, and finally transferred a freshly washed newborn into Diana's arms for the first time.

Diana sat in the chair next to Scottlyn's bed and rocked back and forth. "I've held my share of babies over the years, but this is newest one." She stopped, lowered her nose to the baby's head, and inhaled. "She smells so sweet."

Mercie began to shift and whimper.

"And I think she's getting hungry again."

Scottlyn glanced at the clock over the door. "It's only been two hours."

The older woman stood and passed the baby back to her mother. "Coming into the world in such a hurry must be hungry work." She leaned over and kissed Scottlyn on the forehead. "I'm going to go home and grab a nap. You need me to bring anything back for you?"

Scottlyn snuggled the baby. "Nope, I think I've got everything I need right here."

"Okay, I'll be back a little later."

The door closed behind her and left Scottlyn and Mercie alone for the first time. She stared at the miraculous thing that had come from such sorrow. Love flowed over Scottlyn in warm waves of tenderness. This was her future. From this moment on, very word she spoke, every accomplishment...every breath she took, would all be for Mercie's sake.

BEGGING FOR MERCIE

CHAPTER ONE

"Dead?"

Scottlyn cringed at Marie's reaction to her news. She looked around the crowded library and motioned for her friend to lower her voice. "Yep, almost four months ago."

"Oh wow...How?"

"There was a fight at the prison. The news reports make it sound like he tried to break it up and got stabbed in the process. Bled out before help could get there." Scottlyn shrugged. "I haven't really paid a lot of attention." She had plenty to occupy her mind. *Taking care of a one-year-old, volunteering at the shelter.* She looked at the stack of books on the table. *College in the fall.* "I stay pretty busy."

"I bet you're glad, though."

Scottlyn sat back and looked at her friend with wide eyes. "Marie, that's a horrible thing to say."

"Bradley Nelson raped you. Seems to me that would generate a bit of hate for the person—and glee for the corpse."

Scottlyn stared at her companion. Marie was one of her best friends from Saber High, just back from her first year of college, and obviously out of touch with reality. "He gave me Mercie."

"Well yeah, but—"

"Scottlyn Rich?"

Scottlyn tucked her long blonde hair behind her ear and looked into the face of a stranger. The man was scarecrow skinny. His black suit hung from his shoulders, his white shirt gapped around a scrawny chicken neck. "Yes."

He stretched out his hand, offering her a packet of neatly folded paperwork. Without thought, her hand came up to grasp them. "What...?"

"You've been served."

"Served...what...?"

"You'll find everything you need to know inside," Chicken Neck replied.

The man turned without further explanation, cutting a path around the reading tables and racks of books. The library door slid shut behind him.

"That was weird," Marie said.

Scottlyn nodded. "Way." She unfolded the papers while Marie looked over her shoulder.

"Those look like legal papers."

Scottlyn motioned for her friend to be quiet, reading the top sheet in a whisper. "In the matter of Gabe and Penny Nelson, plaintiffs, versus Scottlyn Denise Rich, defendant. We the plaintiffs wish to petition the court regarding custody of the minor child, Mercie Delynn Rich." The rest of the words blurred beneath nerves and fury. Scottlyn's hands shook as she folded the papers.

"What is it?"

Scottlyn pushed aside the books she'd been studying before Marie's visit interrupted her. She shoved the papers into her bag. Her legs trembled when she stood. "I have to go."

"What...?"

"I'll call you." Scottlyn followed the path of Chicken

Neck's exit and rushed across the parking lot for her red Rav4. Her hands were trembling so badly she had trouble getting the key inserted into the ignition. Her mind refused to take in what she'd read. And what she had read...surely she'd misunderstood. The five miles between the library and home passed in a haze. She jerked the vehicle to a stop in the driveway, raced up the walk, and barreled through the front door. "Diana!"

~ * ~

Diana Kensington, high school teacher, surrogate mother, and honorary grandmother, fastened the tape tabs on a fresh diaper and leaned down to blow a noisy raspberry on Mercie's chubby, bare belly. The baby's laughter bounced off the walls of the room and filled Diana's heart with contentment she'd never known, a level of joy she never expected to be hers.

"You're a chunky monkey."

The baby's cornflower blue eyes sparkled with joy as her little hands lifted. "Up, Gam."

She gathered the child into her arms and sent up a prayer of thanksgiving. *Thank You for giving me such joy.* "I love you, Miss Mercie. This is going to be the best summer break ever, getting to spend every day at home with you!" She looked up when the front door slammed. Scottlyn's urgent call sent her scurrying down the hall with the baby balanced on her hip. One look at the seventeen-year-old's rigid stance and distraught expression brought her up short. "Sweetheart, what's wrong?"

Diana frowned at the tears glistening in the depths of her blue eyes.

"Scottlyn?" The teen's gaze zeroed in on her daughter.

Mercie bounced on Diana's hip, tiny hands outstretched. "Ma...ma...ma..."

Scottlyn exhaled a deep breath, swiped the moisture from her eyes, and retrieved a bundle of papers from the bag hanging on her shoulder. She held them out. "Trade you." She handed the papers to Diana and reached for Mercie with trembling hands. "Come to Mama, baby girl." Scottlyn bundled the child close and paced to the window overlooking the front yard.

Diana watched as Scottlyn buried her head in Mercie's blonde, Shirley Temple curls, and a tell-tale sniff echoed above the baby's excited welcome home jabbering. She sat and unfolded the papers, spreading them out on her knees. Her own agitation grew with each word she read. When she reached the end of the two page document, she folded the sheets neatly and sat back. *The nerve of these people.* No wonder Scottlyn was an emotional mess. She studied her *adopted* daughter. Hadn't the Nelson family brought enough grief into Scottlyn's life? Now they want to take the baby from her? Diana's heart did a free fall to her toes. *And me? Jesus, come bring some comfort to this place.* "Where did you get these?"

Scottlyn stared out the window, her answer weary. "I was studying at the library, trying to get a head start on some of my college courses. Marie came in, and we were visiting. This guy came up to the table and asked if I was Scottlyn Rich. When I said yes, he handed me those papers and left." A sigh shuddered from her lungs. "Do they say what I think they say?"

Diana studied Scottlyn's back. Bringing the pregnant teen into her home seventeen months ago had done more than fill the empty rooms of her house. Scottlyn's presence, and now Mercie's, had given Diana something to focus on other than the grief of her husband's death.

The months of adjustment had seen a hiccup or two, but the two girls fulfilled Diana's abandoned dreams of a family of her own and gave her a new respect for mothers everywhere. She glanced back down at the legal documents in her hand and welcomed herself to another difficult slice of motherhood. "I don't think there's much to misunderstand here."

Scottlyn whirled from the window. "Bradley's parents want custody of Mercie? The same people who denied that their son ever laid a finger on me want to claim my daughter as their own?" Her chest heaved, and the baby struggled against the steel bands of her mother's arms. "Over my dead body."

"You need to calm down."

"Calm down?" Scottlyn's voice was tight with anxiety. "They want—"

Diana forced the suggested composure into her own voice. "What they want and what they get are two different things." She stood and crossed the room. "Let me have the baby before you squish her. It's past her nap time, and I was just about to lay her down. While I do that, why don't you fix a couple of sodas? We'll sit down and see if we can't figure this out."

~ * ~

*How could they...*Scottlyn couldn't even finish the thought. She pulled glasses from the cabinet, filled them with ice from the door dispenser, and poured soda over the cubes. When the warm liquid hit the frozen cubes, their shiny surfaces fractured in a series of spider web cracks. That was her heart. Full of pits and crevices, mostly caused by people she'd trusted. A mother she couldn't remember, a boy out for his own pleasure, classmates who'd turned their backs, the father who'd raised her and tossed her out. Now this. Why couldn't people just leave her alone to raise her daughter?

Scottlyn heard Diana coming down the hall and turned to set the glasses on the table. Her conscience pricked over her maudlin thoughts. Here was someone she could trust. Someone who'd made sacrifices in her own life to ensure that Scottlyn had everything she needed to provide the kind of home Mercie deserved. Someone who'd taught...*and shown*...her more about love and trust in the last year and a half than she'd experienced in her whole life.

Diana entered the room, and Scottlyn threw herself into the arms of the only mother she'd ever known. She couldn't stop the tears. Diana would never ask her to. Wrapped in Diana's embrace, Scottlyn staked a claim on a small island of peace in the storm raging through her heart.

"Diana, can they—?"

"Shh..." With a final squeeze, the older woman took a step back and lifted Scottlyn's chin. "Look at me."

Scottlyn blinked away the tears and looked into blue eyes that were so similar to her own, they could have been related by blood.

"Life is full of cliffs, honey, and people all too willing to give you a push. Let's not give them any more control than we need to." Diana turned her to the table. "Sit down. Let's talk."

Scottlyn allowed Diana to lead her to a chair. "How can you be so calm?"

"Not as calm as you might think. Part of what you're seeing as calm is experience. I've lived a lot more life than you. I've learned to look at things from all the angles before I let them upset me." She stopped to sip her soda.

"This is a disturbing and unexpected fork in the road, but I think you're overlooking two very important things."

"Like?"

"When you were pregnant with Mercie and your father made noises about having the baby taken from you by force, my friend Lynette hooked us up with a paralegal buddy of hers. Do you remember what he told you?"

Scottlyn twisted a strand of hair around a finger while she thought about the conversation more than a year ago. She looked up at Diana, her bottom lip caught between her teeth. "That I didn't have anything to worry about as long as I took care of my daughter, provided for her needs, and kept myself out of any trouble that could be used to prove me unfit."

"And that's exactly what you've done." Diana took in the room with a wave. "You both have a secure home here for as long as you want it. Mercie doesn't need a thing she doesn't have, and you graduated with a 4.0 grade point average. Plus you've been accepted at Oklahoma University. Pretty impressive work."

Scottlyn pushed away from the table, nervous energy driving her to her feet. "But this is different. Dad didn't want Mercie, he just didn't want me to have her. These are grandparents who obviously do want her. Dad never pursued his threat of legal action." She motioned to the papers on the table. "Bradley's parents have. What if they can prove to a judge that they can make a better life for Mercie than I can?"

"You're determined to inch closer and closer to the edge of that cliff, aren't you? You're forgetting the second thing."

Scottlyn stopped and leaned on the back of the chair she'd just vacated. She stared at Diana, waiting to hear something in her favor besides good grades.

Diana sat back and crossed her arms. "Did you dedicate your life to Jesus a few months ago?"

Scottlyn nodded.

"Are you living your life for Him now?"

"I'm trying."

"And trying is all He asks of any of us." She motioned to the chair. "Sit down. Keeping my eye on you while you pace around the room is putting a crick in my neck."

Scottlyn slid back into her seat.

"Sweetheart, do you really think God brought us together, reworked my life and yours, and molded us into a family, just to tear that apart a year and a half later?"

Scottlyn shrugged. "I don't know what to think. I just want to be left in peace to raise my daughter." New tears pressed against the backs of her eyes, and she blinked them away. "Her beginning was brutal and painful. I want to put the bad things behind us and focus on our future."

"And I'd bet money that's what God wants too. But you might have to fight for it. Sometimes God allows these lessons into our lives so we can grow. But you don't have to let fear or worry set the boundaries for the battle." She reached across the table and covered Scottlyn's hand with her own. "God's got this. Regardless of how either of us feels right now, He wasn't taken by surprise by what happened this afternoon." She leaned forward. "Did you say you saw Marie at the library?"

She continued when Scottlyn nodded. "Then Grant should be home from his school in Missouri soon as well, right?"

Scottlyn took a deep breath, calmed by Diana's reassurances and shared faith, warmed by the mention of the journalism student she'd met at church over Christmas break. If you looked up tall, dark, and handsome in a reference book, there was no definition, just a picture of Grant Weber.

Scottlyn took some time over her answer, not wanting to sound too excited about a *relationship* that still didn't quite deserve the term. But the mental image of Grant's cleft chin, crooked smile, and black fringed dark eyes left her all mushy on the inside. "Yeah."

Diana smiled from across the table. "Just yeah?"

The speculative look in Diana's eyes caused heat to flood Scottlyn's face in spite of the upsets of the day. "We're just friends."

"Um hum." Diana held up a hand and counted points off on her fingers. "Friends who've been skyping two or three times a week for five months. He took you and Mercie to his parent's house for their Christmas Eve party. A New Year's date followed, and I believe his parents are on the guest list for Mercie's birthday party in a couple of weeks." She shared a grin. "But we'll go with friends, if that's what you want."

Caught in the net of her own happily-ever-after fantasy, Scottlyn shrugged. She tapped the papers laying in the middle of the table. "What does Grant coming home have to do with keeping Bradley Nelson's parents away from my child?"

Diana sat back and crossed her arms. "What does Grant's father do for a living?"

Scottlyn tilted her head in thought, and a smile spread across her face. "He's a family court lawyer."

"Bingo." Diana pushed the papers a bit closer to Scottlyn. "Why don't you give Grant a call and see when he's going to be home."

CHAPTER TWO

Months after its last cleaning, the abandoned room still carried the musty odor of sweaty boy and well used gym clothes. The single bed was neatly made, junior high and high school sports trophies, dominated by football accomplishments, crowded every available flat surface. A layer of dust coated everything like a light frost on a winter morning. Penny Nelson sat at the desk in the corner of the room, motionless except for the rise and fall of her chest and the steady stream of tears tracking down her cheeks. The tears dripped from her chin where they puddled, unheeded, on the top of the desk.

Her husband, Gabe, wanted to clean the room out. He was afraid she was making a shrine out of Bradley's things. Penny wouldn't allow it. How could he not understand the comfort she derived by being surrounded by the essence of her son?

She stood on shaky legs and wandered around the room, careful not to disturb the slightest fuzz of dust. Memories assailed her, and Penny struggled to sort them out, holding each fleeting moment of her son's twenty-one years close to her heart. Two images took priority in her mind. Her infant son, a strand of her hair wrapped in a tiny fist, snuggled against her breast, drifting off to sleep, and the moment when her hand brushed the hair out of his lifeless face just before his casket was closed the final time.

The same hand clutched the collar of her shirt, and a sob broke from her throat. "How did we get from there to here?" She bolted for the door. Maybe spending so much time here would drive her crazy, just as Gabe feared. Her feet stumbled on the threshold, and she turned for another look. No, she determined. Not a single change. Not until they transformed the room into a nursery.

She startled when a hand came to rest on her shoulder. Gabe's arms wrapped around her, as he lowered his chin to her shoulder, she leaned her head against his.

"Is it done?" she asked.

She felt his nod. "The lawyer's office just called. They served the papers yesterday."

"Good. We need to push for a quick hearing. There's no sense in dragging this out longer than we have to."

Gabe's arms tightened. "Penny, please don't get your hopes up about this. That lawyer you hired was only too happy to take our retainer, but I'm not convinced he can get us what you want."

Penny jerked out of his arms. "Get *me* what *I* want? *Me?*" Her voice grew shriller with every word. She took a step away and pulled Bradley's bedroom door closed with a snap. "What I want is my son, what I'll take is his child. That girl has all the time in the world to have more babies. Mercie is all I'll ever have left of my son." *Mercie. What sort of name is that for a child?* They'd change that once they had custody. *Brandilyn, Brandie?* She faced her husband and swiped tears from her face. "I thought that's what you wanted as well."

Gabe pulled her back into his embrace. "I want what God wants."

Penny struggled against his arms. "God...bah. We

raised our son in church, he was a good boy. Where was God when that girl tempted him away from his beliefs? Where was God when that fight broke out in the prison yard?" Her struggling stopped, replaced with sagging surrender. "Don't talk to me about God. I don't..." Her voice broke, and the rest of her statement dwindled away. She wept into his shirt front.

"You can't say things like that. I know your heart is broken. Mine is too. Every time I walk down this hall, I pause and listen for his music or his laughter. Every time I drive by the school, I try to get a glimpse of the football field, knowing that if I look hard enough, I'll see him." He exhaled a ragged breath. "Bradley was my son too. But we can't blame God for what happened. That's the grief talking." He loosened his hold on her and eased her back to arm's length. "I just don't understand how taking that child from her mother can ease the grief of losing our son."

"You promised to try."

"And you made a promise too, remember?"

Penny's mouth formed a tight line, and she stared at the wall across his shoulder. Her answer was a sharp nod.

"Good, then we're going back to church this weekend?"

"All right!" She took a step back. "Whatever it takes to get you off my back."

~ * ~

Scottlyn slumped against the soft cushions of the couch in the Weber's study. "So they can't...?"

Grant's father smiled. "We have two words for this sort of thing in the legal sphere. Nuisance case. Let me explain a few things." He leaned forward, elbows on his knees, hands clasped between them. "When it comes to custody cases, the law tends to favor the mother unless someone can give substantial evidence that the mother is unfit. I don't think that's an issue here." He nodded to the papers lying on the table between them. "If the judge doesn't toss the case from the get go, I'll be more than a little surprised."

"Then why...?" Scottlyn lifted her shoulders. "I mean, I'm ecstatic that the news is all good. I'll certainly sleep better tonight, but why would a lawyer take a case he can't win? It doesn't make any sense."

Grant's fingers brushed her hand. "I can answer that. Money."

"My son is correct. There are a lot of lawyers out there that give credence to all of those unethical lawyer jokes. The one Mr. and Mrs. Nelson retained doesn't have the best reputation in the county. He's not quite a bottom feeder, but he's close enough. I'm sure that's not what they wanted, and probably not where they started. They probably had to dig deep to find someone willing to give them the answers they wanted to hear for the fee he wanted to charge. Even if the case never makes it into a courtroom, he can bill them for a few hours, claim he did his best, and walk away with a heavier wallet. All nice and legal, because people can initiate a case over anything, but winning that case is another story."

Grant's father seemed so confident. *What if...?* She took a deep breath and did her best to squash the maybes. *If I don't trust him, then why am I wasting everyone's time?* Scottlyn looked from Mr. Weber to Grant and reached for her purse. "You'll never know how grateful I am that you were able to see me tonight. I know it must have been an imposition to meet with me after hours, especially on a Friday night." She withdrew her checkbook. "How much do I owe you?"

"How about an extra slice of cake at Mercie's party next week?"

"Mr. Grant, I'm serious." The lawyer grinned. "Miss Rich, so am I." He lifted a hand when she opened her mouth to object. "All we did tonight was talk. You had questions, I had answers. I'll respond to the complaint first thing Monday morning and list myself as lawyer for the defense. It'll take all of five minutes."

"How long until we hear something?"

"Not long. I'll request the first open date on the docket."

Scottlyn sat back with a smile. "I'll make sure you get a piece of cake with frosting balloons on it."

"Works for me." Grant's father stood. "I'm going to go find my wife. I'm sure you kids can entertain yourselves." He turned for the door.

"Thanks, Dad."

Mr. Weber waved in response and left Scottlyn and Grant alone.

Grant angled to face her. "Are you feeling better about things now?"

"I'm getting there, but there's this little corner of my stomach that's going to be nauseated until a judge rules in my favor." She did her best to reign in her insecurities. "Thanks for the opportunity to talk with him. It's your first night home in five months. I'm sure you had more important things planned."

"Just being with you." He paused. "May I hold your hand?"

Ever the gentlemen, always mindful of her past and the hesitation it bred where men were concerned. *The last time a man touched her...* Scottlyn bit her lip and refused to go there. She nodded.

Grant took one of her hands in his, holding it lightly. "Like I said, just being with you. Mission accomplished."

His words generated a warmth that started at her fingertips, raced up her arms, and plowed straight into her heart. Her pounding heart drove the heat into her face. She stared at the sight of her hand resting in his, waiting for the familiar fear in the pit of her stomach, more than grateful when it didn't materialize. *Thank You, Father.* She met his gaze. "I'm not sure who's the bigger sweetheart, you or your dad."

Grant laughed. "There are times when my siblings and I would disagree with you about that *sweetheart* thing, but Dad's a good sport and a great lawyer. Don't let his mellow attitude fool you. He's a freight train in court. He'll plow Bradley's parents right under the plaintiff's table." He rubbed her knuckles with his thumb. "He won't do that just because he's the best family lawyer in the county. He'll do it because he knows how important you and Mercie are to me."

"Grant—"

"Scottlyn, you're all I've thought about since Christmas break." His free hand joined the one holding hers and sent butterflies tumbling in her stomach. "I couldn't wait to come home. Spending the summer with you, getting to know you and Mercie better, that's all that got me through the last semester." Grant stopped and cleared his throat. "I bought something for you."

Scottlyn lifted her chin a notch and looked at Grant from under her lashes. Her pulse fluttered anew at the emotions she saw reflected in his intense brown eyes. Her heart did a somersault when he ducked his head and gave her a shy grin. Did he have any idea how dangerous the combination of his good looks and shy personality could be?

"You bought me a gift?"

"Yes, and I have a question to ask you." Grant stopped to clear his throat a second time and released her hand to rub his palms along the legs of his jeans. "Scottlyn, I know you're still getting over what Bradley did to you, but I really like you. You have a lot on your plate right now, what with taking care of a baby, Mercie's party, trying to get ready for college, and now this custody thing, but..." He stopped to fumble a small velvet box from his pocket. Scottlyn watched him twist the box in his hands. *What...?*

Grant met her gaze, and she would have sworn she saw a blush staining his cheeks as his expression went from sincere to frustrated. "Sorry." He thrust the box into her hands. "I envisioned this moving a lot smoother."

His muttered words and obvious embarrassment brought a smile to Scottlyn's face and sent the ache of uncertainties scurrying for cover. She turned the box over and over in her hands, finally finding the small latch that released the top. A fine silver chain with a small dangling heart lay nestled on the black velvet. "Grant..."

"Like I said, I know you have a lot of stuff going on, but I wanted to ask if we could...I mean...would you be interested in..." Grant stopped and pulled in a deep breath. He held out his hand and Scottlyn placed the box in his palm. He lifted the bracelet and allowed the light to play on the silver. "What I'm trying to say is that I understand we haven't known each other very long, but I really like you, and I'd like for us to date exclusively this summer and see where it takes us."

Scottlyn held out her wrist. This time the flutter in her heart had nothing to do with Bradly and everything to do with anticipation. Her answer came in a single breathless word. "Yes."

CHAPTER THREE

"No, Liz, I don't think your decision to give your baby up for adoption is the wrong one." Scottlyn's heart nearly broke when she saw the sadness in the fifteen-year-old's wide green eyes.

"Are you sure? I mean..." She stopped to rub a belly that looked ready to burst. "I watch how good you are with Mercie, and I almost think I could raise my son."

Scottlyn glanced around the large library at the Choose Life Shelter. She came here every Tuesday evening to help tutor the students, to try and repay a small portion of the kindness she'd been shown. Tonight the room held a dozen pregnant teenagers, a dozen different stories, a dozen different paths. *Father, please give me the right words.*

She put an arm around Liz's shoulder. "I think it's normal to second guess your decisions this close to your due date, but you need to think with your head, not your heart. You've got two years of school to finish. Your mom's doing everything she can just to provide for you and your sisters. Is it fair to her to add another mouth to feed?"

Elizabeth lowered her eyes and shook her head. Scottlyn saw a tear drip from the younger girl's chin.

"Did Dad's parents change their minds about helping?"

"He's just fourteen..."

Sorrow filled her heart. Parents at fifteen and fourteen. *What had these kids been thinking?* Scottlyn squeezed the skinny shoulders. "Not aborting your baby was the right choice. I think adoption is the right choice too. Didn't you tell me that the adoptive parents agreed to an open adoption?"

Liz swiped her face with the sleeve of her shirt. "They said I could see him at birthdays and Christmas if I want, and they promised to send me a new picture once a month."

Two visits a year and a couple of pictures. Is that what's waiting in my future? Scottlyn swallowed back the bitter thought and put her arm around Liz, focusing on what would be the ideal arrangement for the younger girl. "That's a pretty good plan." She steered Liz to a side table, plucked a tissue from a box, and pressed it into her hand. "I don't want to sound preachy, but I think you need to pray about this. A lot. I know it's hard to think about giving him up, but think about the couple that wants to make a family with him. How will they feel if you change your mind? Can you give him the sort of life they can? I know those are hard questions, but if you listen close, God will give you answers everyone can live with. Do you have your phone with you?"

Liz nodded and dug a phone from her pocket. Scottlyn took it, tapped on an icon, and entered her contact information. She handed the phone back and waited until Liz lifted her eyes back to hers. "You call me any time you need to talk, or even if you just want someone to pray with you."

The younger girl shrugged. "OK."

Scottlyn caught a glimpse of one of the center's directors entering the front door. "I need to run and speak to Mrs. Hatter for a second. I'm praying for you,

OK?"

"Thanks."

She squeezed Liz's hand and hurried out of the room, catching Millicent Hatter on her way to the kitchen.

"Mrs. Hatter, wait up."

Millicent Hatter, Principal of Eden Heights Christian Academy and co-director for the Choose Life Pregnancy Shelter, was sixtyish, slender, and five foot nothing in her stocking feet. Dressed in her traditional two piece suit—tonight's selection a pale peach—she turned in the kitchen doorway and focused a mega-watt smile on Scottlyn. She opened her arms wide. "Oh, come here, dear girl."

Scottlyn stepped into the older woman's embrace and received an almost bone crushing hug. She gave as good as she got. "I miss seeing you every day."

Mrs. Hatter nodded. "Schools only been out for two weeks, but I know what you mean. I always miss my graduates. It's a nice perk that I get to see you here." She held Scottlyn at arms- length. "Has anyone told you, tonight, how grateful we are for your time? Summer school homework is drudgery for most of the girls. A little help goes a long way."

Scottlyn grinned. "Not tonight, but I enjoy it. Coming here gives me the chance to share my experiences. I might even call it selfish, since every girl I help, helps me in return." She looked back down the hall, then leaned in to whisper into Mrs. Hatter's ear. "You might say an extra prayer for Liz. She's really conflicted right now."

"That poor child. Of course I'm praying, but I'll keep an extra eye on her. I know she'll do the right thing when the time comes. Now, come join me for a cup of our horrible institutional coffee and tell me what you've been up to since graduation."

Scottlyn allowed herself to be pulled into the dining room. The older woman poured a cup of black coffee and took a seat at the large table. Scottlyn treated her drink to suitable amounts of sugar and creamer and snagged a couple of napkins and cookies from the bar before she took a seat next to her friend. She handed a cookie across before dunking hers in her coffee.

Millicent Hatter sipped her drink and set the cup aside. "So, what's up with you?"

"Not much, just taking care of the baby and trying to get my college plans in order."

The old teacher grinned, her expression mischievous. She leaned forward. "Really? Just college and baby? I know you young people like to think my generation lives under a rock, but I could have sworn I saw a Facebook notice just last week about you being in a new relationship with a certain handsome journalism student."

Scottlyn met the grin with one of her own. "Saw that, did you?" She held out her arm to display the bracelet. "He gave me this. Called it a token of his feelings." Her sigh filled the room. "He's so romantic...I like it!"

Mrs. Hatter took Scottlyn's hand, turning it this way and that to admire the bracelet. "I imagine so. Romance is almost a lost art these days. You're a lucky girl." She released Scottlyn's hand and pushed back from the table. "I'm sorry to run, but I need to get up to the third floor, we're having a board meeting in an hour, and I have to get our financial report ready."

Scottlyn nodded her understanding. "Don't be late on my account, but I am glad I ran into you." She fished a stack of cards from her bag, flipped through them, and handed one across the table.

"What's this?"

"An invitation to Mercie's birthday party next

Saturday. I was going to mail them out tomorrow. You saved me a stamp."

"Wonderful, I'll be there with bells on." She stood and bent to pick up her cup.

"Don't worry about it," Scottlyn said. "I'll clean up here. You get started on your report."

"Thank you, dear. I'll see you Saturday."

Scottlyn watched the older woman retreat before cleaning up their snack. Satisfied that everything was tidy, she reached for her purse. It was almost Mercie's bedtime, and she needed to get home. The William Tell Overture sounded from the depths of the bag. She fished through make up, pacifiers, and wipes, finally bringing the phone out where she could see it. The number on the screen made her hands shake. Her suddenly nervous fingers stabbed at the icon four times before the call connected.

"Hello."

"Scottlyn, it's Grant's dad. We have a court date set for two p.m. a week from Friday. Can you stop by my office tomorrow after lunch? There are some things I need to prepare you for."

~ * ~

"Hey, check this out."

Scottlyn looked up from a shelf of party favors. Grant stood in the aisle wearing a rainbow-colored sombrero and a plastic mustache attached to goofy glasses. He danced in front of her, heedless of the other shoppers. No one had to tell her that her answering grin was half-hearted.

"Cute." She turned back to the shelf. Mercie's party was tomorrow, and she still had favors, balloons, and ice cream to buy. What sort of favors did you buy for a bunch of toddlers? She sifted through noisemakers, multicolored beads, and small plastic puzzles. *Too many little pieces.*

She felt a presence behind her a second before Grant's arms slipped around her waist. "Scottie."

Scottlyn leaned into the embrace, warmed as much by the nickname as the hug.

"Scottie," he repeated. "I'm sorry. Is there anything I can do to cheer you up?"

She tossed seven small stuffed animals and seven grapefruit-sized plastic balls into the cart. More than she wanted to spend, but hey, it might be the only party she got to plan for her baby, and by George, it was going to be perfect.

A hand waved in front of her face. "Earth to Scottlyn."

She acknowledged his effort with a sigh. How could she make him understand her worry? "The department of child services came to the house today."

Grant took a step back, cocked his head to the side, and reached a hand up to run a finger over the spot between her brows. "That explains the frown."

"Yeah." Scottlyn turned away, grabbed the bar of the cart, and shoved it down the aisle. "Just part of the process." She shrugged. "Your dad warned me that they'd be coming, but it still unnerved me. The lady was nice enough, but I didn't enjoy her poking around the house, and she asked a ton of questions. Where does the baby play, where does she sleep, are there pets in the house, do we have a gate to keep her out of the kitchen?" She stopped and faced him with her hands on her hips. "A pet? I've talked it over with Diana. I was going to get Mercie a puppy soon. Guess that's out of the question."

Grant pulled her to his side. "I'm so sorry they're

putting you through this."

Scottlyn looked up into his serious dark eyes. *Snap out of it girlfriend. You've got a serious hunk by your side, and that social worker didn't find a single thing out of place.* She linked her arm with his and bumped him hip to hip. "I'm the one who's sorry. This whole thing is just...scary, and the biggest reason I didn't agree to a movie tonight. I know Diana enjoys her alone time with Mercie, but I couldn't think about being away from my daughter for the whole evening." She gave him a smile. "I'm done with the mulligrubs tonight. You were sweet enough to understand about the movie and bring me shopping instead. I promise I'm going to try and be more positive."

"How could you not be worried? The outcome of this could change your whole life." He closed his eyes and pressed his palm to his forehead. "That came out wrong. I—"

"You're fine." *This guy...my guy...is so adorable.* "I trust your dad...and God. But I've got to be honest. Every day this drags out...it's just hard not to hate these people."

"Hate is a valid emotion, but by this time next week, it'll all be settled."

Scottlyn closed her eyes and jerked her head into an affirmative nod. She held up a hand. "In my favor."

His hand smacked against hers. "In your favor."

"Then let's make this party happen!" Crepe paper, party hats, and paper ware emblazoned with clowns joined the growing mound of goodies in the cart. Scottlyn smiled as she pushed the cart to the checkout with her right hand covered by his left on the bar. *God, I really am trying to trust You, but I feel so helpless. Thanks for Grant. Having his support on top of Yours makes it a little easier. He's so steady. So not Bradley. I know it's too soon to think about a future with him, but it's hard not to dream.*

They loaded their purchases into Grant's pickup and headed for the local Braum's for the ice cream. Scottlyn hesitated over the impressive selection, finally deciding on a carton of chocolate and one of peppermint. She hoisted it in front of Grant. "Little girls gotta have pink ice cream."

"You're the boss." He nodded to the other side of the store where customers stood in line for burgers and ice cream. "Want a cone?"

Scottlyn's eyes cut to the busy food counter. "Oh yeah. Chocolate almond, two scoops on a waffle cone."

"A woman after my own heart. We'll make that two. You get in this line, I'll get in that one."

They met at the truck ten minutes later. Scottlyn put her bag in the back seat of the extended cab and climbed into the passenger seat before leaning over the console to take both cones so he could climb into the tall cab. They drove in silence, and by the time they got to Diana's house, the summer evening had made her treat a dripping mess. She lifted it and tried to catch an errant drop that was racing down the side of the cone. She surfaced to find a wide grin on Grant's face.

"What?"

Grant pointed. "You've got ...um..." He leaned across the console, cupped a hand on the back of her neck, and brought her close. His head tilted, and his lips brushed the corner of her mouth. "Yum. Chocolate and Scottlyn, what a terrific combination."

The touch of his lips sent an electric jolt straight to her heart. Not the old revulsion attributed to the attack, but a honey sweet hope. She pushed him away anyway. "I have napkins."

"The kiss was more fun."

She stared at him in the fading light, the cone

forgotten, the air in the pickup charged with something that sent goose bumps parading up her bare arms.

"Scottie, you are so beautiful."

She was speechless when he pulled her close a second time and covered her lips with his.

CHAPTER FOUR

Penny jerked the car to the curb and watched the backyard celebration from across the street. It was a perfect day for an outdoor party. A light June breeze stirred the newly sprouted leaves in the tree tops. Mylar balloons floated above the fence from multi colored ribbons. Sunlight reflected from their metallic surfaces. She winced when a stray beam of light speared straight into her eyes, then hunted for a tissue to wipe away the moisture.

No tears today. She shook her head, latching on to the internal denial. Today her Mercie turned a year old. *A year you missed. Twelve months down the drain because you refused to believe...* She forced the thought from her head. *I'm not going there. I can't get the past back, but I can change the future.* In six short days, she would claim Mercie as her own. In six days, maybe her heart could begin to heal. If she could get past this ever present grief she could focus on being the wife Gabe needed and the mother the twins and Mercie deserved. *Mercie.* Penny leaned her head against the head rest, closed her eyes, and crossed her arms. She could almost feel that small, sturdy body pressed against hers. The absence of the reality made her arms and her heart ache with emptiness.

She jerked herself out of the daydream. *Am I losing my mind?* Did crazy people know they were crazy? Tears pressed against the backs of her eyes, and she turned her gaze back to the balloons. *They're not tears, just the light...*

Penny sank down in her seat as another car came to a stop in front of the house. A young couple climbed out. He held a brightly wrapped gift, she stooped back inside and emerged with a toddler in her arms. They made their way to the front door, carefree, confident. Invited.

She fingered the gift on the seat beside her. The sky blue dress with its frilly skirt and puffy sleeves had dazzled her from its place on the rack. She'd raised three sons. Dressing a girl would be a new adventure filled with lace, soft pastel fabrics, and bows. Telling herself to wait a week had been a waste of time. She'd purchased the dress, not knowing there would be a party, intending to leave it at the front door, but now...

Penny turned her attention back to the activity behind the fence. Rage built, shoving the hurt aside for a bit. That was her child...grandchild...and she had every right to be a part of the festivities. How dare they exclude her? She grabbed the package, climbed out of the car, and crossed the street with a confidence born of righteous indignation. She ignored the front door and crossed to the gate on the side of the house instead. They might try to stop her at the door, but the gate offered unattended and immediate access.

~ * ~

Even above the noise of a rowdy chorus of "Happy Birthday," Scottlyn heard the gate hinges squeal. She looked up from the cupcake she'd just placed on the tray of Mercie's high chair. Recognition slammed into her and almost drove her to the ground with its force. The sudden pounding of her heart drowned out the birthday noise, and her vision narrowed to the unwelcome woman, Bradley's mother, crossing the lawn. How dare she? The slim chance that the court might decide in favor of the Nelsons' robbed her of sleep each night, but this was her time. This person would not spoil Mercie's birthday.

Scottlyn handed her camera to Diana. "Get some pictures for me." She hurried across the yard to cut off the enemy. "What are you doing here?"

Bradley's mother stopped and looked around the yard. She almost seemed puzzled by the question. Scottlyn took in the red eyes of her nemesis and the dark circles etched beneath them. The poor woman didn't look like she'd slept in days, or enjoyed a good meal in weeks. Scottlyn shrugged off any trace of sympathy. This was war, and if the first round had to be fought today, then so be it.

Penny Nelson held out the gift. "It's my little girl's birthday."

The term of ownership heated Scottlyn's temper to a full boil. Her hands fisted at her sides, and she had to make a physical effort to unclench her jaw enough to speak.

"You've got a lot of nerve. Leave now, or I'll call the police and have you arrested for trespassing."

Penny lifted her chin and met Scottlyn's gaze. She clutched the gift to her chest like a shield. "I brought a gift. I have every right to give it to her."

A hand came to rest on Scottlyn's shoulder. She glanced back to see Grant. His father flanked her on the other side.

"I'll take care of this." Grant's father stepped around Scottlyn, placing himself between the two women. "I'm afraid you'll have to leave. My client doesn't want you here."

The older woman's face morphed into a mask of

defiance. "Your *client* is on borrowed time. It would save everyone a lot of trouble if she simply gave me what was mine."

I'm going to take this person apart. Scottlyn's nails bit into her palms as her hands fisted in outrage. The only thing standing between her and this...this...delusional *thing*, was the added pressure of Grant's hands on her shoulders.

He bent to whisper in her ear. "Let Dad do his job. She's only hurting her own case right now. Don't let her get to you and make you damage yours as well."

"Mrs. Nelson, you'll have your day in court, but that isn't today. I'm sure your lawyer wouldn't be pleased with your presence here. You're only jeopardizing your case."

Scottlyn watched as Bradley's mother drew herself up to her full height, stepped around the small group of resistance, and marched to the gift table. She placed her present on the stack before turning back to the gate. She paused next to the highchair and brushed a hand across Mercie's curly hair. Without a word she returned to the gate.

"Enjoy the next six days. The rest of her life is mine."

~ * ~

Scottlyn forced her feet to carry her through the halls of the courthouse on Friday afternoon. Diana followed her on the right, Diana's best friend, Lynette Thomas the left. She made it as far as the swinging doors to courtroom three before her feet stumbled to a stop and refused to carry her a step further.

"Scottlyn?"

Diana's whisper barely carried above the pounding of Scottlyn's heart echoing in her ears. "I can't do this."

"Yes, you can." Lynette hissed from behind her. "After

what she did to you on Saturday?" She gave Scottlyn a small shove. "How many times do you need to hear someone tell you that these people don't have a legal leg to stand on? You square up your shoulders, girl, get in there, and claim what's yours once and for all. We've got you're back, and God's got ours. Now move."

Scottlyn pressed her lips into a thin line and straightened her back. Lynette was right. Mercie was hers, and she intended to leave today with that question forever settled. So far, Penny Nelson had fired all the shots in this war. Scottlyn would never forgive her for the way she'd ruined Mercie's party. Well, Scottlyn was no longer on the defensive. She was ready to fire some shots herself."

She pushed through the doors and marched up the center aisle, pausing only long enough to take Grant's outstretched hand for a second as Diana and Lynette scooted into seats next to him.

She met his gaze. The confidence on Grant's face bolstered her courage a notch further. She nodded at him and hurried to take her seat beside Mr. Weber at one of the tables on the other side of the railing. Across the room, Bradley's parents sat with their lawyer. His mother's posture was stiff, her face a mask of grief. She didn't even glance in Scottlyn's direction.

Scottlyn waged a solitary battle with tears she refused to shed in the face of the enemy. Anger began to build in her heart, and she embraced it. *Good!* She'd take anger over fear any day of the week.

Mr. Weber leaned in to whisper in her ear. "You OK?"

Scottlyn shrugged. She started when his hand come to rest on top of the ones she held clenched in a white knuckled ball on top of the table.

"Relax. You've got nothing to worry about."

"Can you promise me that, because—?"

"All rise. In the matter of Nelson versus Rich, let all parties come forth to be heard. Court is now in session, The Honorable Miles Alexander, presiding."

Chairs scooted, clothing rustled, and no one seemed to breathe as the door behind the judge's desk swung open to admit a tall man dressed in a black robe. He took his seat and tapped the microphone with his index finger. "Be seated."

The judge looked over the small group. A deep exhale echoed from the courtroom speakers as he dug a pair of glasses from a hidden pocket, cleaned them on the corner of his robe, and settled them on his nose. "I've read all the documents presented to me by the lawyers in this case. I'm ready to make a ruling." His eyes cut sharply to his right, focusing on the plaintiff's table, and taking on an expression of sincere sympathy. "Mr. and Mrs. Nelson, while the court can understand your deep-seated grief in this situation, you have failed to provide any proof to your allegations that Miss Rich is an unfit mother. The home has passed inspection, and the mother's background check returned to the court spotless. The defendant offers the child a stable home and is a caring and attentive parent."

Judge Alexander's gaze moved to rest on Scottlyn. "Miss Rich, The court openly apologizes for any discomfort the pursuit of this case may have caused you. I can't pick and choose which cases I adjudicate, but I can do my best to see that justice is served in my courtroom."

He straightened behind the desk and raised his gavel. "The court finds in favor of the defendant." The sound of the gavel echoed through the room, restoring Scottlyn's breath. "Case dismissed."

A low moan started from across the room and built to a scream. "Dismissed?" Bradley's mother jumped to her feet, sending her chair clattering into the railing behind her. She shoved the restraining arms of her husband out of her way. "How can you dismiss us without even listening to what we have to say?"

She turned and pointed a trembling finger in Scottlyn's direction. "She sent my son to prison and cost him his life. How can you say she's a fit person to raise our grandchild? That child is all I have left of my son." She stumbled back, sank into her chair, and rocked back and forth while tears coursed down her cheeks. "She killed my son."

Scottlyn watched in horrified silence as Bradley's father gathered his wife into his arms and practically carried her sobbing figure out of the courtroom. Her gaze followed them out. *I killed their son?* What about what their son did to me? If my daughter lived without grandparents this year, it's their own fault. If they'd just listened, if they'd just made an effort to be a part of her life.

Diana rushed through the swinging wooden gate that separated the spectators section from the defense table. Scottlyn found herself enveloped in the older woman's arms. "It's over, Scottlyn. No more worries. Let's go get the baby from the sitter and have a nice victory lunch."

Scottlyn nodded, but she couldn't tear her eyes from the door. *She killed my son.* Somewhere beneath the relief and joy of the judge's dismissal, a small kernel of sympathy tugged at her heart.

Grant's arm's came around her next and she found that kernel completely smothered by the jubilant look of victory on his face.

CHAPTER FIVE

The table and the candy dish rattled like thunder in the dark room. Scottlyn bent over, righted the dish with one hand and with the other, rubbed her bare shin where it had connected with the sharp corner of the coffee table. She grimaced at the noise and the pain, training her ears for sound from behind the closed doors of the bedrooms down the hall. Nothing stirred. Satisfied that everyone except her still slept, she turned from the doorway and resumed her midnight musing.

The lights in the room flashed on. Scottlyn swallowed a yelp, spun back to the hall, and found Diana in the doorway, a can of pepper spray aimed and ready. The women stared at each other for a second.

Scottlyn drew in a long slow breath.Diana lowered the can.

"You scared the life out of me," Scottlyn said. "That makes two of us. What are you doing banging around in here in the dark, at"—she glanced at the clock on the mantle—"two a.m.?"

So much for working out my thoughts in peace and quiet. "I can't sleep. When I get like that, lying in bed just makes me more restless, so I pace. I was trying to do it quietly."

The older woman slid the can into the pocket of her robe, crossed the room, and brushed a strand of Scottlyn's hair out of her face. She cupped her chin. "I thought relief would have you sleeping like a baby tonight."

Scottlyn lifted a shoulder and stepped around Diana. "You'd think so, wouldn't you?" She bounced a fist off her thigh. "I just can't get her expression out of my head."

"Bradley's mom?"

"Yeah, and it's weird. I mean...she's a crazy woman who tried to steal my child. She's out of my life and Mercie's for good, signed, sealed, and legal. So why should I lose any sleep over her?" She turned and lifted her hands in surrender. "But every time I close my eyes, there she is."

Diana nodded and took a seat in one of the room's overstuffed chairs. "Why do you think that is?"

Scottlyn stared at her feet while the clock on the mantle ticked the night away. She faced Diana and scraped the hair out of her face with an unsteady hand. "Because crazy wasn't all I saw."

Diana cocked her head and waited.

"I saw grief, and I saw longing, and I saw love. Crazy I could deal with. But those other things? How am I supposed to ignore those?"

Diana held out her hand. When Scottlyn crossed the room to take it, she pulled her down to sit on the arm of her chair. "Sweetheart, Maybe God is trying to show you something more."

"What?"

She waved the question away. "I can't listen for you, and I can't tell you what to do, but I can tell you a story."

"A bedtime story? I've outgrown those, haven't I?"

Diana grinned. "Call it what you wish. But I bet you find something important in it." She settled back in her chair, and her eyes took on a dreamy quality.

"Small towns can be very insular. They don't always

run at the same speed the rest of the world is addicted to. Sabor is no exception."

"Diana, this isn't news. I've lived here all my life."

She patted Scottlyn's leg. "Yes, but you haven't lived as much life here as I have, so cut me a little slack. I'm the one telling this story."

Scottlyn shrugged and waited for her to continue.

"Small town life can be a good thing and a bad thing. Churches of all denominations, public schools and private, community activities...the lines can get a little blurred, but that's part of the charm. If you live here long enough, you'll meet almost everyone, and almost everyone will, through acquaintance or grapevine, know you and your story." Her words trailed off as she stifled a yawn.

"Sorry. I'm glad Mercie will be your alarm clock in the morning, not mine. Anyway, about fifteen years ago Sabor's city council decided to hold an annual celebration. They wanted to draw in some commerce from the neighboring towns while getting residents, old and new, involved in something that fostered some renewed civic pride. It was a massive undertaking. They planned a rodeo, a parade, a gospel sing, a craft show, a farmer's market, and a street dance. A real carnival atmosphere complete with games for the kids and food vendors for the grownups. They decided to call it—"

"The Sabor Roundup," Scottlyn supplied. "It happens every year in August. I've attended it my whole life." *And what does any of this have to do with Bradley Nelson's mother?*

"But you weren't there for the first. That first year, it seemed like everyone in town had a job to do. Sabor's public schools partnered with Eden Heights to put together a fund raiser to benefit both schools. We had a couple of nice raffle prizes and a bake sale. Joe Anderson brought three of his young horses in and sold pony rides. A couple of the other farmers got together and supplied some baby animals for a petting zoo."

"We still do all those things." Scottlyn said around a yawn of her own.

"Yes, but we only did the pageant the first year."

"Pageant?"

"Yeah, someone wrote a play about the founding of Sabor. It was a hoot and more fiction than fact, but the whole town got behind the production. It was going to be the diamond in the crown of the first Sabor Roundup. With kids in both schools participating and the gospel sing right afterwards, most of the town turned out that night.

"The play centered around Marcus Sabor and his family's struggle to carve a living on the harsh Oklahoma frontier. Marcus established a homestead and opened a general store and, before long, more businesses opened and more families moved into the fledgling town. Marcus went off to fight in the Indian Wars and never came home. Mrs. Sabor rose from the ashes of her grief to found the first school, named for her late husband. And from those humble beginnings Sabor, Oklahoma, was born." Diana shrugged. "Like I said, as productions go, it was pretty cheesy, but there was one little actor who absolutely stole the show that night." Diana paused and squeezed Scottlyn's hand.

"A little boy with black curly hair. He couldn't have been more than four, and he couldn't remember his lines for squat, but he had the cutest smile, no one in the audience seemed to care. His mom stood just off the platform with twin baby boys asleep in a stroller by her side. She spent the whole hour practically shouting his lines to him. And where some parents would have been embarrassed at their child's failure," Diana made air quotes around the word, "her face simply glowed with more love and pride than I've ever seen."

Scottlyn's stomach filled with heaviness even as her eyebrows lifted in realization.

"I never met that woman, but I've never forgotten the look on her face. Today, we both saw a face filled with grief and pain. But under those things, I couldn't help but see the memory of a young mother's love and pride in her son."

~ * ~

Scottlyn spread a blanket under the brilliant violet blooms of a redwood tree in Sabor's tiny city park. A few feet away, Grant pushed Mercie in a baby swing attached to one of the sturdier limbs.

"Diana didn't know?"

Scottlyn set out their picnic lunch of sandwiches, chips and fruit, and shook her head. "She told me that she never met them, never knew their names. She thought she recognized Bradley's Mom the day she crashed the party, but she wasn't sure until the day of the hearing."

"That's amazing." He stopped the swing. "You ready to eat, Squirtling?"

Mercie kicked her legs and bounced in the seat, doing her best to set the swing back in motion. "Go!" The baby's single word was followed by a jutting lip and a liquid blue gaze.

Scottlyn laughed at the look of helplessness that washed over Grant's face. "You're gonna have to toughen up, or she'll have you wrapped around her little finger so tight, you won't be able to breathe."

"But look at that face."

"Ignore the face, it's a weapon."

Grant tilted his head and frowned in confusion.

Scottlyn sighed. "Oh, good grief." She fastened her eyes on Grant's face, rounded them into pleading circles, and forced her lips into a little pout. "Grant, will you let me pick the movie tonight...please?"

He looked from one pouty face to another. "Wow, you're good."

"We're women. *The look* is imprinted on our DNA in the womb. Mercie is a particularly fast learner."

"So I should ignore the face?"

"From her, never from me. Pluck her out of there and let's eat."

Grant did as she requested, bringing the squirming one-year-old to the blanket. Scottlyn set her down in front of a bowl full of halved green grapes. Mercie's protests over being removed from the swing died as she buried both hands in the squishy green fruit.

"Is she eating or playing?"

"A little bit of both, I hope. Now that she's feeding herself, meal times are an adventure for both of us." Scottlyn smothered a yawn and handed Grant a plate. "Sorry."

"That's OK. Did you get any sleep last night?"

"Not much. There's just so much in my head. I don't know what to do. Especially after Diana's story."

"What's left to do? Everyone had their day in court. The judge ruled in your favor. Problem solved, case closed."

"Maybe, maybe not." She looked at Mercie and had no defense against the wave of love that flooded her heart. "If it were just me, I probably could walk away from this whole thing and be done, but when you add Mercie to the equation, it gets a whole lot more complicated."

"In what way?"

Scottlyn took her sandwich apart and layered potato chips on top of the sliced ham. She smushed it back together. "Right now, Diana and I"—she glanced at Grant from under her lashes—"and you, we're Mercie's life. But she won't always be a baby."

"I'm not sure what you mean. You guys aren't going anywhere, and if you'll let me, I plan to hang around for a really long time."

She looked into his eyes. Her heart warmed at the promise she heard in his words. "Oh, I'm keeping you, but I'm talking about later. I never intended to give Mercie the gory details of her conception, but I didn't plan to keep her in the dark about her father, either. He's gone now, and she's going to have questions as she grows that I can't answer. How do I explain things to her if I've cut the people with answers...her grandparents... out of her life?"

Grant frowned. "I don't get it. You just went to court to keep these people out of her life."

"No, I went to court to keep custody of my child. But the whole thing made me realize that her grandparents might have some rights as well. Their son made some bad choices, but that doesn't make his parents bad people. Should I keep them out of my daughter's life as punishment for what Bradley did? That doesn't seem like a very Christian way to live."

"Mama."

Scottlyn looked down. Mercie was covered in a sticky glaze of grape juice, but the bowl she held up was empty, the smile on her face full of accomplishment.

"Gone gone."

Scottlyn took the bowl. "Look at you. You are such a big girl." She opened a package of wipes and focused on cleaning the messy hands and face.

Grant reached over and brushed a few smashed grapes from the blanket. When he continued, his voice was tense. "I was just as excited as you were about the outcome of the hearing the other day. What if I said that I have feelings for you and hopes for our future? Plans that don't include Bradley or anyone connected to him."

Scottlyn took a fresh shirt out of the diaper bag, shook it out, and pulled it over Mercie's head. "That could be a problem since, you can't take Mercie or me out of that equation." She met his gaze across her daughter's head, taking in the storm of negative emotions gathering on his face. "I like you a lot, and I'm honest enough to admit that having any sort of relationship with Bradley Nelson's parents is not my first choice. But if that's what God is telling me to do..." She shrugged. "Then I'm just going to have to suck that up. And so will you."

Eight hours later Scottlyn paced the living room dressed for her dinner and movie date with Grant. He was two hours late and hadn't called. Her temper teetered on the edge of eruption. She looked at the clock a final time. Two hours wasn't late, it was not coming. Two hours late without a call of explanation was stood up. Her hand hovered over the phone, and she jerked it back. *Bradley ruined my life and my dad kicked me out. I will* not *give another man control of my emotions!*

She fingered the bracelet on her wrist and heard Grant's words. *"I know you have a lot on your plate right now."*

Yes, she did, and there was no room left for a temperamental man.

CHAPTER SIX

"Penny."

In that strange place between awake and asleep, Penny shifted on the mattress, turning to hug a pillow close. "Shh. I just got the baby back to sleep."

"Baby? What...?"

Gabe's question jerked Penny up. She rolled to the edge of the bed and blinked in the harsh overhead light. "Is he awake again?"

From his place in the doorway Gabe drew his hand down the length of his face. "Penny, why are you sleeping in here?"

"Bradley was crying earlier, I hope he's just teething, but..." Penny stopped and looked around the room. No baby, no crib, no rocker, just trophies, dust, and memories. She dropped her head into her hands as a wave of reality capsized her dream world. Her shoulders shook in silent sobs as she rocked back and forth. *Not teething...dead.*

The mattress dipped when Gabe sat beside her and gathered her into his arms. "Sweetheart, you've got to stop this."

She leaned into his embrace, more tired than she ever imagined she could be, her voice as empty as her heart. "Stop? How can I stop loving my baby? I miss him so much."

"I'm not asking you to stop loving him." Gabe paused and held her away so that they were eye to eye. When she focused on his face, the pain she saw reflected in his expression almost made her flinch. She closed her eyes, determined to believe that no one could share the depth of her anguish.

Gabe shook her shoulders. "Penny, look at me. This isn't healthy." He smoothed the hair from her face, his voice a whisper when he continued. "You're killing yourself a day at a time. We lost Bradley. We both have to find a way to live with that, but it feels like I'm losing you too." He gathered her close again and buried his face in her hair. "I can't lose you. I need you. Jared and Joel need you."

The shelter she found in her husband's embrace acted like a candle in a windowless room. Penny rested against him, content when the shadows of grief retreated to the darkened corners of her soul, if only for a little while.

"I know you're worried," she said, "and I'm sorry, but I don't know how to fix what's broken. Sometimes my heart hurts so much it scares me." Her voice dropped on a sigh. "I was never made to outlive one of my children."

His hand moved up her back to stroke her hair. "I can't tell you how to grieve, but you have to realize that you aren't going through this alone. You have me and the twins. We can get through this, but we have to work at it together."

Together? Locked in the solitude of her grief, she didn't know what that meant anymore. Shame pricked her. She was almost relieved that Joel and Jared were off in Montana on an archaeological apprenticeship. She was in no shape to be a mother to anyone just now. A moment of rationality made her cringe. *And whose fault is that? You spend your days locked in this room. They just graduated, and left.*

Do you even know what their plans are for the future? The honest no that echoed through her thoughts dragged a fresh sob from her throat. Her husband's arms tightened, and she clung to him like a lifeline. *Steady, dependable Gabe.*

The comfort of his arms gave her a boldness she hadn't felt in months. "But I'm just so angry." That single acknowledgment opened the flood gates on emotions she'd been unable to express aloud. "Not just angry, furious." She shoved her way out of his arms, stood, and took a few steps away from the bed. "I'm mad at that girl for enticing my son away from his beliefs. I'm mad at Bradley for being foolish and getting himself killed. I'm mad at the judge for denying me what should be mine. I'm mad at myself for so obviously failing my son. I'm mad at God, because I know He could have prevented it all." Penny faced Gabe with her hands on her hips, her rant coming to an end. "And I'm mad at you."

He tilted his head, his tone uncertain. "Why are you mad at me?"

"Because you aren't as mad as I am. I want you to be angry too, but instead you've got this...peacefulness about you. It's like you've forgotten Bradley ever existed. It infuriates me."

"I'm not even going to justify that with a response." He studied her for a few seconds. "I've been angry, and it didn't change a thing." His sigh hung in the air along with her accusation.

"When the scandal of the rape first broke, all I wanted to do was hide." He leaned forward, braced his elbows on his knees, and stared at the floor. "Every place I went I was sure people were whispering about Bradley and what a failure I must be as a father. I mean really, how did my son learn to treat a woman...a girl...like that if he didn't learn it from me? I bought into the whole ugly package;

anger, guilt, and shame. So much shame that when you decided you couldn't face our friends at church, I followed you right out the door." He held his hand out to her, dropping it slowly when the gesture went ignored. "I owe you an apology."

"For what?" she snapped.

"For accepting Satan's lies. For not being the husband you needed. For being led instead of leading." He stood and stepped in front of Penny, placing his hands on her shoulders. "But that ends today."

Penny narrowed her eyes. "What do you mean?"

"I've reclaimed my faith. It's time for you to do likewise."

Penny tried to take a step back but found herself held firmly in place. "Faith, smaith. Did you hear what I said? I'm mad at God. It's all religious mumbo jumbo. If there was an ounce of truth to it, our son would still be alive."

"I'm not going to accept that nonsense any more than God will. We had a deal. I let you slide out of your promise to go back to church with me last week. I knew you were anxious about the hearing, and I didn't want to put any more on your plate. I was wrong. Starting today, its Joshua 24:15 for me."

"What's that supposed to mean?"

"As for me and my house, we will serve the Lord."

She shook free. "You can't force me—"

"You're absolutely right. I can't force you to do anything you don't want to do, but you gave me your word, and you've never lied to me. Do you plan to start now?"

Penny crossed her arms. "It's a waste of time. There's nothing there for me."

Gabe's expression was just as militant as her posture. "Maybe not. I know I can't give you peace or the answers you so desperately need, but I can put you in a place where you can find them." He stopped to look around Bradley's room. "Because I promise you that you won't find them here. I've got a new church picked out for us this morning. Now go get dressed."

~ * ~

Sunday mornings at Sabor's Faith Tabernacle began with fellowship and ended with prayer. The members of the congregation bridged the gap between start and finish with Sunday school, an exuberant session of praise and worship, and a timely and always thought-provoking sermon from Pastor Robbins.

Scottlyn made the transition from Sunday school to the sanctuary. She took the long away around, avoiding the nursery. Mercie was in a clingy stage. If she saw her mother between services, the baby would make life miserable for the nursery volunteers. Each parent had a number, and if their child needed special attention during service, that number would be discreetly displayed on the projection screen behind the pastor's head.

She hurried up the aisle to take a seat next to Diana. Her gaze found the back of Grant's head and, as if by some sixth sense, he glanced in her direction. Scottlyn met his gaze head on. He ducked, but not in time to hide the red that stained the tips of his ears. *Good, I hope he spends the next hour squirming in his seat.* It would be a just reward for the night she'd spent tossing and turning, trying to decide if their future was dead before it even got started.

The praise and worship team took their places on the platform, and the congregation scrambled to their feet as the piano struck the first notes of the opening chorus.

From the pocket of her jeans Scottlyn felt the vibration of an incoming text message. She pulled it free for a quick glance.

I'm having the baby. Can U come?

Liz. Scottlyn took a deep breath. Diana's car was in the shop, so they'd ridden together this morning. Leaving now would mean Diana missed service as well, but she'd made a promise to the younger girl and she wouldn't break it. She nudged Diana's arm and held the phone up so she could read the message.

"I have to go."

"Of course you do. Just give me a few seconds to write my tithe check and drop it in the offering. I'll meet you at the nursery."

Scottlyn nodded, scooted out of the pew, and left to claim her daughter. She leaned over the half door and watched as Mercie wrapped a stuffed monkey in a baby blanket. "What you got there, baby girl?"

Mercie scrambled to her feet, monkey forgotten. "Mama!" She ran to the door on her stubby legs and held up her hands. "Mama, up."

Hailey Bowan was serving dungeon duty for the morning service. She faced Scottlyn with her hands on her hips. "Now you've done it."

"That's OK. I'm here to pick her up. We have to cut the morning short."

Mercie bounced in place while the door was unlocked. Hailey picked her up, moving a few steps back so Scottlyn could get the door open without knocking the excited toddler to the floor. The baby strained out of Hailey's arms trying to reach her mother.

Scottlyn pulled her into her arms and dropped a kiss on the top of her head. "Mama missed you."

Mercie snuggled her head on Scottlyn's shoulder, stuck

a thumb in her mouth, and patted her mother's back with her free hand. "Home?"

Scottlyn laughed. "Yes, we're going home just as soon as your grandma gets here."

"I'm here."

Scottlyn turned back to the door to find Diana waiting. "I'm so sorry you have to miss service because of me."

Diana shook her head. "I'll survive. Babies take precedence."

"Who's having a baby?" Hailey asked.

Scottlyn snagged Mercie's diaper bag off the hook on the wall. "One of the girls at the shelter. She's giving her son up for adoption and asked me to be there for moral support."

Hailey shook her head, sympathy evident on her face. "That's got to be tough. She's lucky to have a friend like you. I'll be praying."

"Thanks." Scottlyn bundled Mercie close and left the nursery with Diana at her side. "I hate to take the car and leave you guys without transportation for the rest of the day."

"We'll be fine." Diana said. She held the heavy glass door open, allowing Scottlyn to lead the way to the parking lot.

Scottlyn stopped short just outside the door. Bradley's parents stood on the other side of the covered drive.

"You!"

The single word spewed from Penny Nelson's mouth as she took a surprised step back. Her expression twisted with visible rage. Her nostrils flared and her eyes went wide. Scottlyn knew the woman's formidable temper was about to erupt. She tried to take a step forward and found her feet glued to the pavement. She felt Diana's hand on her back.

"Mr. and Mrs. Nelson, we were just leaving."

Bradley's mother broke the standoff. "I've no doubt of that. I'm sure you were told to get out. A murderous slut and her...her keeper."

Mr. Nelson put a hand on his wife's shoulder. "Penny."

She shook it off. "You've got no business in the house of God." Her gaze traveled to Mercie and in a heartbeat morphed from fury to longing. "And you have no business raising that child. I'm not done. It's just a matter of time before I can convince a judge that she belongs with me."

The woman's venomous words lent steel to Scottlyn's back and shoulders. She straightened. "You're pathetic." The words left her mouth without thought, and something in her conscience pricked her. "I'm sorry, I didn't mean that, and this isn't the time or place for a confrontation." She took a deep breath and leveled her gaze at her nemesis. "I never wanted to take sides against you or anyone else, but since you've drawn the battle lines, you should know that it won't be an easy fight. And that's a shame. It would have never crossed my mind to hold you responsible for your son's actions. If you had asked to be a part of Mercie's life..." She shrugged and allowed her words to dwindle away. She hitched the strap of the diaper bag up on her shoulder and tightened her arms around her daughter as the baby began to fuss, obviously distressed at the loud words. "Just stay away from us, please. I'll get a restraining order if I have to."

She jerked her head toward the parking lot where her Rav4 waited, trusting Diana would follow. A scuffle behind her caused her to turn.

Penny Nelson struggled against the restraining hands of her husband, doing all she could to lunge in Scottlyn's direction. "Don't you walk away from me! And don't you dare feel sorry for me. I don't need sympathy from a tramp like you."

Scottlyn turned her back without answering, crossed the road to the car, and used the remote to unlock the doors. The car seat was on the passenger side. She handed the baby over to Diana and scrambled into her seat. Her hands shook as she pulled the door closed. Penny Nelson's tirade and the word "slut" filtered through the windows and rang in her ears.

CHAPTER SEVEN

Penny drifted. On their return to the house after church the day before, Gabe insisted she take a sedative to calm her nerves before putting her to bed. She had no idea what he'd given her, but she knew there was a pharmacy to choose from, remnants of the numerous failed attempts at counseling since Bradley had died. Part of her fuzzy brain seemed to remember waking in the night, engulfed in tears and misery. She thought there might have been a second pill at that point, followed by her husband's strong arms, and murmured words as he rocked her back to sleep. *Words...had he been praying?*

Joints popped as she stretched. Gabe was a good man. *Better than I probably deserve right now.* Memories of her behavior yesterday surfaced in her groggy brain, and she cringed. *Did I really say those horrible things?* She buried any thoughts of remorse in a deep hole next to her son. She refused to be sorry for her outburst. Her son was dead. Someone had to bear the blame. When she flopped onto her back, sunlight angled through the slats in the blinds and stabbed her eyes. Penny blinked. *How late is it, anyway?*

A loud thump from down the hall distracted her from thoughts of the time. She lay still and tried to isolate the sound. When it came again, dread and fury filled her in equal portions. She tossed the covers aside and raced down the hall to Bradley's room. The view from the open doorway froze her feet to the floor. One word scrambled from her brain and lodged in her throat with no sound. *No!*

Bradley's bed had been dismantled. The sheets and bedspread lay in a pile on the floor. The mattresses, headboard, and frame leaned against a wall no longer decorated with sports posters. She swallowed, finally finding her vocal chords.

"No!" She stumbled into the room, picked up the bedding, and held it to her chest. Sobs shuddered through her body. Her words erupted in a shrill scream. "What do you think you're doing?"

A weary sigh came from the inside of the walk-in closet. Gabe stepped into the light, holding a bundle of Bradley's clothing in his arms. When he raised his head, Penny saw tears on his face. She ignored them. How dare he violate this space?

"Exactly what it looks like. I'm cleaning out Bradley's room." He swiped his face on the wad of clothes, and his harsh cough filled the room. "It's time to move on with our lives."

"Time to...what are you talking about?"

Gabe moved into the room and dumped the clothes into a box. When he looked up, Penny stepped back, away from the resolve she read in his expression.

"We can't live like this anymore." He dragged his fingers through his hair. "I've said that so much, I'm beginning to sound like a broken record." Gabe held his hands out in an open invitation. "Look at yourself, Penny. When was the last time you had a haircut?" He motioned to her clothes, and she pulled the baggy T-shirt she'd slept in around herself. "You're nothing but skin and bones. When was the last time you ate a decent meal, or had any interest in doing anything other than sitting in this room?" He looked at the clock sitting on the dresser. "It's two in the afternoon. You've been asleep for almost twenty four hours."

Penny straightened. "I was asleep because you drugged me."

"I drugged you because you were hysterical from the scene you caused outside the church." He met her gaze. "Our. Son. Raped. That. Girl."

"No, she—"

"Did nothing." Gabe interrupted. He paced a few steps away, dragging his hands through his hair and down the length of his face. When he turned his eyes implored her for understanding. "The least we owed Scottlyn Rich was enough indifference to allow her to live her life in peace. Instead, we've done nothing but make her life a misery." He looked at the floor, then returned his gaze to her, straightening his shoulders. "Have you forgotten that she wasn't the only one? What about that nursing student who made the same accusation? Are you going to stand there in your delusional self-righteous grief and tell me that they *both* lied?"

He gave her a moment to respond, and continued when she didn't. "No answer? Can you dig down under your grief for just a second and think about the rest of us? You've allowed your anger to cut you off from everyone around you. You have two other sons and a husband who need you. Jared and Joel will be home from their Montana trip in a couple of days. They've been gone since they graduated, you haven't asked about them once. We should be getting their stuff ready for college, planning a welcome home party."

He raised his hands in supplication. "Our twenty-fifth anniversary is in October. What about our plans to celebrate in Cancun, to have the honeymoon we never got to have?"

"How can you be so selfish?"

"I don't call it selfish, I call it done. I'm not living in a mausoleum for another day. We both go back to counseling in the morning."

Penny turned away from her husband. The disarray of the room cut her more deeply than the truth of his words. "Gabe, please don't do this. Help me hang up Bradley's clothes and put the bed back together. I'm not ready to let him go."

Her husband's impatient sigh sounded heavy in the room. "Why can't you hear me?"

"You don't—"

"Pick three things," he told her.

"What?"

"I know you need to grieve, and I know you need to keep him close while you do. Pick three things to keep here. The rest is going into storage just as soon as I can get it packed away and a facility rented."

She looked around the room, rocking in place and tugging at the hem of her shirt. Panic squeezed the breath from her lungs. "We have an attic."

"And you think I'm going to put everything up there so you can simply change the location of your daily vigil? Think again."

"Gabe..."

Her husband shook his head. "I love you, Penny, and I loved our son, but Bradley is gone. You have to learn to live with the fact that he isn't coming back."

The bed clothes fell to the floor when Penny raised her hands to her ears. "Don't say that!"

"Penny—"

"No!" The single shouted word echoed in the room. She turned and raked her hand over the top of the dresser. Her action sent trophies and high school memories crashing to the floor. Her furious steps took her to the bookcase. She cleared the shelves in four swipes. Penny stood in the middle of the mess, her chest heaving with sorrow and exertion.

"I hate you!"

"And I love you."

His soft response deflated her temper. Penny lowered her gaze to her feet, shoulders slumped, emotions spent. A scrap of cloth protruding from the mess on the floor caught her eye. *What...?* She stooped to pull it free. The books fell away to reveal a worn receiving blanket. Faded dinosaurs frolicked in a forest washed almost colorless by numerous laundry days. *Bradley's blankie. He kept it all these years.* A tremor began in her heart and spread to her fingertips. She closed her eyes and saw her little boy dragging the blanket from room to room like a character in a comic strip. She remembered the days he sat on a stool in front of the dryer, waiting for it to come out clean and warm. *I thought we'd have to make socks out of this silly thing to keep him from dragging it to school.*

Penny raised the worn flannel to her nose and inhaled. All trace of her son was long gone, replaced by the dust of too many years. *Oh baby, where did I go wrong?* A muffled sob escaped into the room, and her knees threatened to buckle. She turned for the door.

"Penny?"

She ignored her husband and continued down the hall with the blanket clutched in her arms. She pulled her purse off the hook by the door, climbed into her car, and drove.

~ * ~

Scottlyn stood at the window of the nursery, her arm around Liz's shoulders. She was beyond weary. Liz's baby had arrived at eight the previous evening, healthy and screaming his lungs out. An event that should have been joyous but was instead filled with tears as Liz and her mother held each other and discussed, again, the impossibilities of raising the child. It was two more hours before Scottlyn was able to pull away and get home to Mercie. Once she slept, nightmares haunted her dreams. Visions of life without her daughter, brought on either by Liz's heartbreaking situation or Penny Nelson's threats.

Useless threats. She'd spoken to Grant's father again today. Embarrassed to seek him out, but reassured by what he'd had to say.

She took a deep breath and forced her brain to focus on the here and now. Beyond the glass wall, newborns rested in clear acrylic bassinets. The window was crowded with proud parents showing off their newborns. One couple stood to the left, arms around each other, whispering softly as their eyes lingered on their brand new miracle. Scottlyn smiled. Next time she'd do it right, sharing every bit of the nine month journey, and the joy at the end, with a husband. *Maybe Grant...*She stopped the daydream in its tracks and returned to the here and now. She scanned the last names on the cards and finally found the one she was looking for. The dark haired baby boy was fast asleep, his lips moving in unconscious sucking motions. She squeezed Liz's skinny shoulders. "You did good."

"He is beautiful, isn't he?"

"Absolutely perfect." Scottlyn bit her lip, almost afraid to ask. "So...did you decide to hold him?"

Liz shook her head and pressed her mouth into a hard line. "No, just looking at him is hard enough. If I held him..."

Scottlyn turned the younger girl from the window and steered her to the bank of elevators further down the hall. "Let's go back to your room." She kept her arm around her friend as they walked and waited for Liz to take the lead in the conversation.

Liz shook free when the elevator door began its silent glide shut and stuck her hand out to stop the door. She leaned through the opening and gazed back down the corridor. The longing on the younger girl's face almost broke Scottlyn's heart. A few days removed from the fear of losing her child by force, she could only imagine the emotions involved in giving a baby up by choice. *Father give her strength.* "We can go back for a few minutes, if you're not ready to leave."

Liz pulled herself up straight. "No. I asked them to put me on a floor other than maternity so I wouldn't be so close. I have to let him go." She stabbed the button for the next floor up. "He's being circumcised this evening and going home with his...parents... first thing in the morning. I think they're releasing me tomorrow night." Her brave façade evaporated, and she sagged against the wall of the elevator. "Can you come spend the morning with me tomorrow? I don't know what I'll do if I'm by myself, knowing that my baby is going home without me."

"Your mom—"

"She couldn't afford to take any more time off work." She shook her head. "Never mind, you've done enough. I'll be OK."

"Yes, you will, because I'll be here by eight. I'll bring us some chocolate milk and donuts for breakfast."

"Thanks." Liz looked at Scottlyn with tears gleaming in her eyes. "Nothing in my life has ever been this hard.

My heart is so tangled up. Do you think things will ever go back to normal?"

The door dinged open before Scottlyn had to answer that impossible question. Liz led the way back to her room while Scottlyn offered up another silent prayer for wisdom. The younger girl settled herself in the hospital bed and collapsed on a stack of pillows.

"I used to run for fun. I can't believe how tired a short walk down the hall makes me."

Scottlyn released a sigh of relief when it seemed as if the question of *normal* was off the table. "Having a baby is hard work. You'll need to take it extra easy for the next couple of weeks."

Liz nodded her acceptance. "So?"

Oops...guess I didn't dodge normal *after all.* Silence stretched while Scottlyn tried to form an answer. She finally lifted a shoulder. "I don't think *normal* ever applies once you've had a baby, regardless of what happens afterward. It does something to your heart that can't ever be undone. That's probably not the answer you wanted, but I won't lie to you."

Liz's head fell back on the pillows, and Scottlyn saw two fat tears slide down her cheeks. She sat on the edge of the bed, took one of Liz's hands, and squeezed. "I wish I could help more."

Liz returned the pressure. "I know I'm doing the right thing, but it feels like my heart is being ripped out by the roots."

"I promise it will get better. I know how empty those words sound right now, but you have to give yourself some time to heal, physically and emotionally. By the time school starts, you'll be ready to get back to the theater classes and track meets that you love so much. There's a rumor that the drama club is planning a production of My

Fair Lady." She paused, leaned forward, and brushed Liz's long dark hair from her face. "With your figure and voice, you're a natural for the lead in that."

Liz shrugged.

Scottlyn pressed on. "You'll be old enough to drive soon, too. How many months until you have your license?"

"Three." The younger girl's voice remained listless and unanimated.

"See, you've got lots to look forward to. It'll be Christmas before you know it."

Liz's face crumpled. "And I can see my baby."

Scottlyn sighed in defeat. It seemed as if every detour she took was doomed to circle back to the same topic. "Yes, you can see your baby." She tried a final time to cheer up her friend. "How about we plan a shopping trip? I'll help you pick out some gifts for your baby."

Liz scrambled from her prone position and pulled Scottlyn into a desperate hug. "Spencer. They named my son Spencer."

CHAPTER EIGHT

It took thirty minutes for Penny to work up the nerve to get out of the car once she reached her destination. She spent that time gathering her resolve and looking out over the tidy expanse of green grass. The clumps of colorful flowers dotting the landscape might have said garden to some. All it spoke to her was a soul deep misery. *This is a waste of time.* She nodded, admitting to herself the validity of the thought. But so much of the last four months...longer if she started counting from the day of *that girl's* initial accusation... had been wasted on negative and unproductive emotions. What did one more afternoon matter? One thing rang true in her heart. She'd fallen as far as she could afford to. *I have to start climbing out of this hole, and I am the only one who can take that first step.*

With a final exhale of determination she collected what she needed from the seat beside her and opened the door. Bird song flooded her ears, further reinforcing the sense of a garden. She did her best to block the cheerful sights and sounds. This wasn't a place for cheerful, this was a place for tears. Maybe if God were willing, today it would be the first step in healing.

If God were willing? The thought had tears pressing against her eyes. Her family and Scottlyn Rich weren't the only ones she'd mistreated. *God, I've been so wrong. If you're still there for me, please help me do this.*

She turned back to the car and tugged four large, helium filled balloons free, careful not to burst them on the door frame. The light spring breeze sent the red orbs twirling and had the attached ribbons tangled before she completed the twenty steps to the bench. *Twenty steps...it's amazing how your mind latches onto the mundane when you can't face reality.*

Penny sat, the same breeze still twisting the balloons on their ribbons lifted the hair from her neck and sent the brand new leaves on the trees above her head dancing in the sunlight. The shifting patterns of shadow and light reminded Penny of her heart the last few months. Moments of clarity mixed with despair. *No more. Please God, no more.*

She fastened her eyes on the headstone of her son's grave. If one's life truly was measured by the dash between the dates, then Bradley's life had been too short. To most of the outside world, he'd be remembered as a nameless young man who raped *that girl* and later died in prison. Penny refused to define him in that way, choosing instead to cling to the countless memories of a mother and her first born.

"You were such a good boy. I remember the day you were born as if it were yesterday. Just one of thousands of babies born into the world that day, nothing special in the grand scheme of things, but when our eyes met for the first time, you changed my life forever." The hand that wasn't busy taming the balloons held the baby blanket to her heart.

"I became a mother. Responsible for your behavior, proud of your accomplishments, and totally in love with every breath you took." A brisk burst of wind tugged at the balloons and drew her attention upward.

I love you in just the same way, daughter.

The words echoed through her heart and brought a sad smile to her face. She took a deep breath. *I can do this. I have to do this.* She turned back to the grave marker.

"Do you remember when you were eight-years-old and your puppy died? You were so heartbroken. I couldn't seem to do anything to put a smile back on your face. You spent days moping around the house and picking at your food. There were days when you sat next to that small mound of dirt in the back yard, just bouncing Dover's nasty tennis ball while tears ran down your face. After a week or so of that, you came running in the house one day and asked me to take you to buy some balloons. You wanted to send a message to Dover." She brought the bright red balloons down to bounce in her lap.

"When we got home you took those balloons and wrote messages on them. I love you. I miss you. Good dog. A few I don't remember. You took them outside, stood by that tiny grave, and released your thoughts to the wind. You didn't come back inside until they floated completely out of sight. Once you were done, you never cried for Dover again."

Penny put the blanket aside and juggled one of the balloons free. There were four, all in the brightest red she could buy to represent the fury of the emotions she was battling. There wasn't any healing in the balloons, but it was a symbolic start.

She'd written messages on all four. The one she chose first read GUILT. She fixed her son's face in her mind. "Bradley, I love you. I'll never forget you. I can't promise that I'll never cry for you again, but you made your own choices. I'm not responsible." She released it. The color was glaring against the blue of the sky. She allowed her eyes to follow its progress until it disappeared from view.

BLAME came next. ANGER. Then GRIEF. She

prayed as she watched each one float away. "Father, I'm so sorry. Please take these things I can't live with any longer out of my heart and leave the sweet memories of my child and the comfort of your lasting love and peace."

Penny settled back on the bench and watched until the last red dot winked out of sight. She stood, took a deep breath, and walked back to her car. Her fingers trailed along the top of the marker as she passed. It was time she went home. Gabe would be worried. She had things to share with him and an important errand for him to run.

~ * ~

The doorbell rang.

"Scottlyn can you get that, my hands are covered in flour."

Scottlyn looked up from her place on the floor next to her daughter when she heard Diana's muffled request from the kitchen. "Got it." She laid the doll aside and scooped Mercie up and into her crib. "Wait right here, baby," she said and ran to answer it. The moment she pulled it open, she found herself engulfed in Grant's arms.

"Scottie, I'm so sorry. Does admitting I'm a colossal idiot count as an apology?"

Unable to raise her head, she spoke into the front of his shirt. "Ifs a part." The words were unintelligible, even to her.

Grant released her from his embrace and held her at arm's length. "I didn't hear what you said, but you haven't kicked me off the porch, so I'm going to take that as a good sign."

Scottlyn crossed her arms and lifted her chin. "I said, it's a start. And the only reason you're still on the porch is that we seem to agree on the idiot question."

He ducked his head, and Scottlyn pressed her lips into a stern line to keep from giving into the smile that tugged at the corners of her mouth. *That embarrassed blush is so adorable.* "So...you're an idiot..."

"And I'm really, really sorry. I was wrong to stand you up. I was wrong to think I could make decisions for you and Mercie. I don't deserve to have such an incredible woman in my life. If the time ever comes in our relationship where I can be a part of the decision making process for Mercie's future, I promise we'll handle it together with mutual prayer and discussion." Grant stopped to take a breath and finally looked up. "Those decisions are *not* all about me and what I want. We both need to listen to what God wants for her and us."

"Wow." Scottlyn tilted her head and studied him. "It's only Monday. You figured all that out in just three days?"

"Three days of thinking on my part and the silent treatment from my mother." He shrugged. "She likes you almost as much as I do. I haven't had a hot meal since she found out I stood you up. If you don't forgive me, I might starve."

Scottlyn studied the dismal look on his face, taking time with her thoughts before spelling it all out for him. "It's not just me that's taking a risk here. If we continue to see each other you have to understand that Mercie, young as she is, has a stake in this too. I can't be with someone who's going to jerk either of us around. I'm a big girl, but I won't have my daughter hurt. I like you, but I'll live the rest of my life alone if that's what it takes to keep her heart safe."

Grant nodded. "I do understand that." He reached up and tucked a strand of her hair behind her ear. "I'm an idiot, like I said, but part of that is because I have feelings for you. *Like* is too mild a word, and it's too soon to call it love, but..." He spread his hands. "I'd never hurt either of you intentionally. Will you give me a second chance to prove that?"

Scottlyn searched his eyes. He met her gaze without flinching, obviously waiting for her to tell him to go or stay.

"You haven't had a hot meal in three days, huh?"

"Mom can be vicious when she's trying to teach me a lesson."

This time when she felt a grin threaten, she gave in to it. "You're forgiven. Now come in the house. Diana's cooking dinner. I can fix that hot meal deprivation thing." She turned to open the door and looked back when he didn't follow. She jerked her head toward the front room. "Are you coming?"

"I bought...I mean...I have a surprise for Mercie. I didn't want to bring it in until I knew you didn't hate me." Grant rolled his eyes. "I don't mean hate, exactly." He motioned for her to stay put. "Just wait right here for a second, OK?"

Scottlyn nodded. Grant turned, jumped from the porch, and raced to his truck. She watched as he extracted a box from the passenger seat. He came back up the walk holding the box flat in one hand, the other hand balanced on the top. *Is he holding the lid down?* She studied man and gift. When he reached the porch, she heard the scrabbling of nails from the box and leaned down to listen. It wiggled and she jumped back. *Hamster or guinea pig?*

She blocked the door and frowned. "Let me just go on record here. If there's a rodent in that box, you're a dead man."

Grant's face fell. "You don't like rats?"

Her jaw dropped. "If you bring a rat into this house, I

won't have to kill you. Diana will do it for me."

Grant chuckled and leaned to plant a kiss on the end of her nose. "No rats, and the contents of the box have been Diana pre-approved."

"Diana knew you were coming?"

"Some surprises require thought and pre-planning. Now, would you let me in and go get Mercie. I promise, it's a good surprise." The scratching from the box intensified. "Albeit an impatient one."

~ * ~

Scottlyn left Grant standing in the living room and went to fetch Mercie. She detoured into the kitchen. "Grant's here, but I'm thinking you expected him to drop by."

Diana grinned, turned the fire down under the chicken she was frying, and grabbed a dish towel for her hands. "Yea! Go get the baby."

"What—"

"Scoot." She glanced back at the stove. "And hurry. I've got about ten minutes before I have to be back in here. I don't want to burn dinner, but I don't want to miss the surprise."

Scottlyn threw her hands up in surrender and continued to Mercie's room. She stopped in the doorway. She hadn't been gone ten minutes. Mercie had escaped the crib. The one-year-old sat on the floor surrounded by a dozen baby dolls. The baby and the dolls were all stark naked."

She crossed her arms and leaned against the door facing. She was raising an exhibitionist Houdini. "Baby girl, what are you doing?"

Mercie looked up with a radiant smile. "Bath?"

Scottlyn shook her head, stooped to pick up her daughter, and grabbed a diaper from the stack by the crib. "You're a mess, but it's not bath time yet." She fastened the diaper and retrieved Mercie's discarded shirt. "You want to see Grant?"

Mercie squealed, flailed her arms, and kicked her chubby legs on the changing table. "Gant...Gant!"

She smiled down at the excited little girl. "I'll take that as a yes." Scottlyn scooped her up and bundled her off to the living room. She found Grant and Diana on the sofa, the lid off the box and their heads together, whispering excitedly. "Will someone please tell me what's going on?"

Grant slammed the lid back into place, handed the box to Diana, and reached for Mercie. "Come here, Squirtling." He plucked the baby from Scottlyn's arms and lifted her high over his head. "I missed you. Have you been a good girl?" His question was answered with a string of baby gibberish. He lowered her to the floor. "Wow, that good, huh?" He reached for the box and sat it next to the curious child. "Can you open it, Mercie?"

Fresh from a round of birthday presents, Mercie knew the drill. She scrambled to her feet, grasped the bow on top of the box, and pulled the lid free. She leaned over to peer inside and raised round eyes to her mother. She sat hard on her diapered bottom, tipped the box onto its side, and clapped her hands. "Baby!"

Something small, black, and curly scampered from the box and attacked Mercie's bare toes with a tiny pink tongue. The baby's laughter filled the room.

Scottlyn hurried to sit next to her daughter, scooping up the excited ball of fur. She held it close and the little tongue went to work on her nose. "Oh..."

Grant joined them in the floor. "She's a teacup poodle, almost eight weeks old and well on her way to being house trained." He put the puppy back on the floor, and she immediately left the adults and scampered back to play with Mercie. "Mom has a friend who raises them. You mentioned you were thinking about a puppy. I thought this little lady might be the perfect fit. She's on loan for the evening, pending mommy approval." He laughed when Mercie toppled to the floor with the puppy on her chest. "Just so you know, I have a kennel and everything else she needs in the back of the truck."

Scottlyn shook her head. "It's a generous gift." She looked at Diana. "You're good with this?"

Diana angled her head toward the two babies playing in the floor. "How can I say no to that?" She stood to return to the kitchen. "Watching them grow up together will be an adventure."

Grant stood and offered a hand up to Scottlyn. They sat on the sofa while Mercie and her puppy continued to get to know each other. He rested his arm on the back of the sofa and propped his left ankle on his right knee. "Hey, Squirtling, can you tell me her name?"

Mercie jabbered, the only intelligible word in her response was "baby."

Scottlyn laughed as she settled in the curve of Grant's outstretched arm. "I think she's named her baby, Baby."

Grant tightened his arm, pulling Scottlyn closer to his side. "I'm glad you're OK with this...and everything. Let's promise never to fight again."

The pup backed up a short distance from Mercie, lowered her head, raised her hindquarters, and barked at her new human. Mercie rolled into a crawl and mimicked the pose and the bark.

When Scottlyn recovered from the fit of laughing, she wiped her streaming eyes and patted Grant on the knee. "I don't think promising never to fight is very practical.

How about if we promise to make up quickly instead?"

"Speaking of." Grant placed a finger on her chin and turned her head to face him. He met her eyes, and Scottlyn felt her heart plunge to her toes. Her jumbled brain registered his intent a second before his lips joined hers. They jumped apart like guilty children when the doorbell chimed through the room.

Grant groaned, and Scottlyn scrambled to her feet. "Hold that thought."

CHAPTER NINE

Scottlyn fanned her hand in front of her face as she walked, trying to dissipate the heat of Grant's almost kiss. Anxious to get back to the living room to make their near miss a reality, she reached for the knob with an annoyed mumble. "This better be important." The door swung open. She felt a frown settle on her face and didn't even try for remorse. After the events of the last few weeks, Scottlyn didn't figure anyone would blame her. She crossed her arms, an immovable force in the doorway. A she-bear guarding her cub.

"What are you doing here?"

Bradley's father looked as uncomfortable as she felt. He scraped a hand through his hair and cleared his throat before he spoke. "I know I'm not a person you want to see on your doorstep. After everything we've put you through, I don't deserve to ask, but I have to. May I have five minutes of your time?"

Scottlyn stared at him at a loss for words. A look over his shoulder and into the car parked at the curb confirmed that he was alone. *Wonder where the crazy woman is?* She finally found her voice. "Umm...just stand right there. I'll be right back." She closed the door in his face and hurried back to the living room. Diana joined her from the opposite direction.

"Dinner's ready. Who was that at the door?"

Scottlyn closed her eyes and used two fingers to rub at a spot above her right brow. "Bradley's dad. I...uh...left him standing on the porch. He says he wants to talk to me."

Grant got to his feet. "I'll send him packing if that's what you want me to do."

Scottlyn shook her head. "Thanks, but I don't think he's here to cause any trouble. Maybe if I hear him out, he and his wife will go away for good." She looked around the room. "Diana, will you take Mercie to the kitchen and get her started with dinner? Grant, secure the puppy, but I really would like you to sit with me while he says his piece."

Diana nodded and bent to lift Mercie. "Let's go eat, angel."

The puppy, deprived of her human toy, plopped down and closed her eyes. Grant scooped her up and put her back in the box. "She'll be all right there for a few minutes."

"Thanks, guys." Scottlyn turned back for the door. *Maybe he gave up and went away.* When she opened it the second time, Bradley's father stood there, waiting patiently. *So much for wishful thinking.*

With dread building in her stomach, she swung the door wide, motioned him in, then scooted around him and led him to the living room. "Feel free to sit if you like." Her words weren't the most gracious, but she didn't know how to fix that.

Mr. Nelson sat on the edge of one of the loveseat cushions and leaned forward, his head down, his hands clasped between his knees. His posture telegraphed nervousness. *Well, join the club.* Scottlyn took a seat on the sofa next to Grant. She didn't bother to introduce the men, and she didn't pull away when Grant took her hand.

The warmth bolstered her courage.

Bradley's father began his speech without preamble and without looking up. "I came here to tell you how sorry I am for what we've put you through. Bradley's death...well, it hit his mother and me pretty hard. If there's a right way to handle something like this, we've been slow to find it. My wife thought she could find some peace by replacing our son with your daughter. I love her enough, and I feared so deeply for her wellbeing, that I allowed her to try. I know now what a mistake that was."

Bradley's father raised his eyes, and Scottlyn's breath caught in her throat. She'd never seen such despair on the face of another human.

He reached for a small bag that Scottlyn hadn't noticed until now. "I have something for you...well, for Mercie actually. I hope that you'll save it for her until she's older." He removed a folded square of fabric from the sack. "We found this today when we were cleaning out Bradley's room. It belonged to him when he was Mercie's age."

He laid it on the coffee table, and Scottlyn rose to pick it up. She spread the nubby flannel blanket across her lap. "Someday Mercie will have questions about her father. What he did to you was inexcusable." His soft words carried a note of pleading. "But maybe when the time comes to tell Mercie about him, you can temper what you say to her with the knowledge that he wasn't always the monster you knew. He was a good boy who made a bad choice."

"Mr. Nelson, I..." Scottlyn stopped, forced to clear the emotion from her throat. Whatever she had expected from him, it wasn't this.

"Scottie?"

She smiled at Grant but shook her head at his silent

question. "Mr. Nelson. I can't take something like this. It holds too many memories."

"You're right, it does, but we want Mercie to have it." He stood. "That's all I came to say. That and to let you know that Penny has agreed to see a counselor. You don't have a reason to believe me, but she isn't a bad person either, just grieving. I promise you won't have any more trouble from her."

Scottlyn got to her feet as well. How could she just let him walk out? She searched her heart for something she could do to lessen his grief. "Would you like to meet your granddaughter before you leave?"

Despite the longing on his face, he shook his head. "Nothing would make me happier, but do you understand how hard it would be to see her once and never see her again?"

Images of Liz weeping outside a nursery window flooded her mind. *She made a choice to walk away, to do what was best for her baby.* Respect for the man in front of her grew a little. All Scottlyn could do was nod.

"I know we sort of blew our chances where Mercie is concerned. But maybe someday..."

Scottlyn's heart pounded at his words, and the pressure in her chest stole her breath. *Jesus, what do I...?* She held her hand out to him. "Call me. When someday comes, and you feel like the time is right, call me. Maybe we can pull all the bits and pieces of Mercie's family together to make a whole." She wasn't sure where the words had come from, but their release restored her breath.

He nodded and hurried from the room. She heard the door close behind him and turned to find Grant standing behind her. The pity on his face mirrored hers. She had no idea what she should do next.

Dinner took a sharp detour from the celebratory atmosphere of young love restored, turning solemn as Scottlyn related the details of Mr. Nelson's visit.

Diana swallowed and dabbed at her lips with a napkin. "So, what happens next?"

Scottlyn pushed food around on her plate, appetite gone. "That's a really good question." She looked across the table. Mercie sat in her highchair, doing her best to feed herself dinner, wearing more mashed potatoes than she'd managed to consume.

"And I don't have a good answer. The rape was the worst thing that ever happened to me." She smiled when Grant laid his hand on hers. "But Mercie...she's the best thing that ever happened to me. I meant what I said to the Nelsons Sunday morning." She stopped. *Was that really just yesterday?* "I never thought about it one way or the other. But if they'd have come to me and asked to be a part of Mercie's life, I don't think I'd have said no. Mercie will want to know about her father someday. Who better to share those things with her than her grandparents?"

"And now?" Diana prompted.

Scottlyn shrugged. "I don't have a problem with Mr. Nelson. But Bradley's mom creeps me out. Above and beyond what I might be inclined to do out of sympathy, I have to protect my daughter. I'm praying, but I don't seem to be getting any answers."

Diana pushed her plate to the side and leaned across the table. "I think you could learn a few things from the story of Joseph."

Scottlyn frowned, searching the list of Bible stories she'd learned in the last year and a half. "The guy whose ten older brothers sold him into slavery?" She shook her head. "You're going to have to explain that one."

Grant nodded as well. "To me too, Mrs. Kensington. I probably know that story better than Scottie does, but I don't see the parallels."

"I don't doubt that. Sometimes it's hard to see the truth when you're standing in the middle of the fight. But, follow me on this. Joseph was betrayed by the very people who should have loved him the most. People he trusted to do him no harm. Their jealously ripped him from everything he loved. Then once he was settled in a new home, with a new position of respect and responsibility, the devil took that away from him as well and he landed in prison. But Satan couldn't keep God from blessing Joseph. He was in prison but he still rose to a position of leadership. He became the respected trustee and interpreter of dreams."

Scottlyn smiled. "I think I get it. Even though people I've trusted, mainly my father and Bradley, betrayed me. God turned their betrayals into blessings. My home here with you and my life with Mercie. A future I would have never dreamed of on my own."

"Exactly," Diana said, "and now, just like Joseph, you've faced another trial. This whole custody thing was Satan's way of trying to take away the new blessings you've found in your life. It could have defeated you, but you held onto your faith and came out a stronger person." She titled her head and grinned at Scottlyn. "I was so proud of the way you handled Bradley's mother yesterday. I don't know that I could have dealt with that situation with nearly as much grace as you did."

"Oh, I don't know if I'd call it grace. I was just too mad to think of anything to say." She waved that aside and got back to Diana's story. "But, when you put it that way, I guess I see your point. I still don't know what happens next, though. In the story of Joseph, his brothers came to see him, and he moved them all to Egypt." She propped her elbow on the table and rested her chin on her fist. "I don't want to live with Bradley's parents."

"I don't either, but maybe what you're hearing as no answer to your prayers is God's way of telling you to wait. Just like Joseph had to wait."

"For what?" Scottlyn shook her head. "Now I'm confused again. What did Joseph wait for?"

"Sometimes you have to read between the lines of Bible stories. I don't think there was a lot of love lost between Joseph and his brothers, but don't you think he missed his father and his younger brother? Do you think he worried about what his father thought had happened to him?"

Scottlyn looked at Grant.

He shrugged. "Don't ask me."

Scottlyn turned back to Diana and shrugged. "Probably?"

Diana laughed. "Well, I'd say, judging by his reaction to his brothers once he recognized them and the questions he asked, he was very concerned about the people he left behind. But think about it. By the time his brothers came to him for food during the famine, Joseph had been in a position of authority in Egypt, second only to Pharaoh, for eight or nine years. Even if he couldn't get away from his responsibilities to make a trip on his own, he could have sent a messenger to his father, someone to let Jacob know that he was alive and well and then bring back word of the family. But the questions he asked his brothers would indicate that he never did that. The Bible doesn't say, but I bet God and Joseph had multiple conversations on that subject, and I think God's response was always 'wait'."

"And I'm waiting for...?"

"For the time to be right, sweetheart. I think you were spot on when you told Bradley's father to call you. God needs some time to work on all the hearts and lives involved in this messy situation. Bradley's parents need some time to get their grief under control. Time for his mother to get the help she needs. Time for both of them to renew their relationship with God. I think, just like Joseph's brothers, they'll come to you once those things happen. Then you can take your final lesson from the life of Joseph."

Scottlyn sat back and looked at her daughter. "Because I'll have what they need."

"Exactly. When the time is right, they are going to want a relationship with you and your daughter, and just like Joseph, you'll hold all the cards. You can turn them away, and after what you've been though over the last two years, no one would blame you." Diana stopped to offer the baby a bite of chicken from her plate. "Or you can choose the higher ground and extend a little Mercie."

CHAPTER TEN

Six months later

Penny waited until she heard Gabe's car leave the driveway, abundantly thankful that the local Air Force base had placed their employees on a mandatory six day shift for a few weeks. With the sound of her husband's engine fading into the distance, she threw the covers back, rolled from the bed, and hurried to her closet. Today had to be the day. The door swung open, and she grabbed the first clothes she could find. What she wore wasn't important. All that mattered was that after a week of fruitless watching, today might be the day that *that girl...Scottlyn...* broke her routine and left the house without Mercie.

She grabbed the bag she'd packed a week ago, bottled water, a book, and a package of peanut butter crackers, and pulled it from its hiding spot. The action dislodged a box hidden behind her clothes. Penny picked it up and studied the doll encased behind the thick plastic of the packaging. It almost looked like Mercie with its blonde curls, pink little bow of a mouth, and blue eyes. Her heart twisted with longing. *Please God, let today be the day.*

She shoved the doll back into the dark recesses of her closet. That and the rocking horse from last month's craft show would be the perfect Christmas gifts for her granddaughter. Gabe knew nothing of the gifts, or her

167

daily surveillance of Scottlyn Rich. He wouldn't approve, but Christmas was just two weeks away, and she had to act now if she wanted to spend any part of the holiday with Mercie.

Dressed for the day, she paused outside Bradley's room on her way to the kitchen. Six months after Gabe's decision to put Bradley's stuff in storage, the room remained empty. Every time she walked by the closed door, the plans she had for Mercie flooded her mind. Gone were the initial visions of a nursery. Her granddaughter was eighteen months old now, a little girl instead of a baby. She would need a toddler bed, not a crib, a toy box in place of a changing table. Penny had the furnishings all selected, including a rocker for bedtime cuddling, paint for the walls, and a lovely pink floral wallpaper border that would take Mercie into adolescence. Gabe would have called her plans premature, but she was ready.

She laid her hand on the door and spoke aloud to the memory of her son. "Bradley, I still miss you beyond words. I've accepted that won't ever change. It is better, though. I don't cry as much. I've gained back most of the weight I lost. Your father and I have gone back to church. He tells me almost every day that he's proud of my progress. I hope what I'm about to do doesn't backfire and change his mind." With a final pat on the door, Penny continued on her mission.

She parked her car three doors down from her target at eight o'clock on Saturday morning. The red Rav4 was still in the drive. She'd watched the house from a different location every day this week, alternating vehicles between her car and an old work truck Gabe hardly ever drove. She didn't need to be reported for trespassing and have the cops breathing down her neck.

The girl's routine hadn't varied all week. Every morning Scottlyn Rich left the house at seven with a book bag over one shoulder, a diaper bag over the other, and Mercie in her arms, bundled against the December cold. She strapped the child into a car seat and drove to a popular and well-secured daycare center. Each day, mother and child went in, and only mom came out. The thought of Mercie spending her days in such an impersonal environment ate at Penny's heart. She didn't work, so she could easily provide the daily care Mercie needed. If she had her way that situation would change for the better shortly.

For five days Penny had returned home empty handed. The daycare wasn't the place for a confrontation. This was a delicate plan, best accomplished one-on-one. Surely Saturday would bring the break in Scottlyn's routine that she needed.

By ten in the morning, Penny was almost ready to concede defeat and wait for another day when motion from the house up the street brought her out of her daydream and put her on full alert. The girl approached the Rav4 alone, climbed into the driver's seat, and backed out of the drive. Penny's heart pounded with anticipation, and her hands shook on the steering wheel as she maneuvered her car into position. The bright red SUV was easy to keep in view, so she dropped back several spots. She had no clue where they were going, but she vowed to have the situation resolved by day's end or her name wasn't Penny Kathryn Nelson.

She followed the Toyota into the lot of a popular toy store and managed to snag a parking space two rows from where Scottlyn parked. Penny watched the girl enter the large building. She grinned. *Christmas shopping for my granddaughter, no doubt.* She grabbed her bag and followed the girl into the store. It was time to make her move.

~ * ~

Scottlyn pushed a cart through aisles stuffed with toys of every kind. She'd left Mercie with Diana so she could shop for a talking bear Mercie had seen on TV, but the wide selection of baby dolls sidetracked her quest. Heaven knew Mercie didn't need another toy, but what would Christmas be without a new doll under the tree? She reached for a princess doll from a favorite animated movie. A noise behind her had her spinning around with the doll clutched to her chest. She did a double take when she saw who stood beside her cart. Her stomach tumbled, heavy with foreboding. "You."

Bradley's mother smiled. "Sorry. I didn't mean to startle you, but you're a hard person to catch alone. I've been looking for a chance to talk to you all week."

The skin on the back of Scottlyn's neck crawled with goose bumps at what the woman's words implied. "All week? Have you been following me?"

"Nothing so sinister as all that. I have something I want to give you."

Scottlyn took a step back when Penny Nelson's hand slipped into the bag hanging from her shoulder. Her apprehension changed to surprise when she pulled out a small photo album. "Pictures?"

Penny nodded. "I didn't want to come to your house. I was afraid you wouldn't let me in. You'd be justified in that. I didn't want to approach you when you had Mercie with you. I didn't want you to think seeing her was my only motive." She held out the album. "I finally felt like going through some old pictures. I know Gabe brought Bradley's old blanket to you. I hoped you'd consider putting these away for Mercie as well." She raised the book an inch higher. "Please."

Scottlyn took the book and studied the woman standing in front of her. Her eyes were clear and free of tears, her hair neatly styled. Her clothes no longer hung off her shoulders like a deflated mannequin, the remnants of a tan lingered on her face and arms. All in all, she looked pretty normal. Not at all like the crazy woman in the church parking lot spewing barbed insults.

"Thank you." Penny whispered.

Scottlyn nodded, not sure where either of them went from here. She didn't wonder long.

"Could I ask you for one more favor?" She waited for an answer, eyes downcast, the fingers of one hand twisting the rings on the other.

She's as nervous as a worm in an aquarium full of hungry fish. Diana's words from six months ago surfaced in Scottlyn's mind. *They'll come to you when the time is right.* Was this the time? "What can I do for you, Mrs. Nelson?"

Penny looked up. "I was wondering..." Her voice wavered, and she stopped to swallow as a couple of other shoppers wandered into the aisle. "This isn't the best place to talk. There's a Starbucks across the street. Once you've finished your shopping, I'd love to buy you a hot drink." There was just a hint of pleading in her voice when she continued. "I don't deserve to ask, and you don't owe me a thing. I'm not even going to ask you for a definite answer. Just think about it while you shop. I'll be there, waiting for you until noon."

Without giving her a chance to answer, the older woman turned away and hurried down the aisle and out of sight. Scottlyn returned to her shopping, but the activity lost some of its appeal. *What does she want to talk about, and why should I listen?* One doll and a talking bear later, she still hadn't decided what to do.

She took her purchases to her car. "Father, what do You want me to do? They've been quiet, You've been quiet. Things are perfect in my life right now. Mercie's growing like a weed. Grant will be home for Christmas break in a few days." She refused to let her thoughts dwell on the gift she hoped she'd be getting from the handsome journalism student. But if her mind wandered to small, black velvet boxes, she rarely bothered to pull it back. *We'll be the picture-perfect little family, the poster children for happily-ever-after.* She pulled her thoughts out of fantasy land and focused on the woman waiting across the street. "I don't want to rock the boat, but I don't want to ignore your direction either." Scottlyn looked at the green and white sign across the street. "Please tell me what I should do." She settled behind the wheel and waited for several minutes. Nothing happened. *I guess no answer is a no.* She started the car and backed out of her spot. Before she pulled out of the lot she got a sudden craving for a white mocha cappuccino. She shook her head and laughed out loud. "Well, alrighty then."

Scottlyn entered the coffee shop ten minutes later and spotted Bradley's mother at a table by the window, reading a book. She looked up when the door chimed, and Scottlyn saw her mouth move in silent words. Words that looked a lot like *thank you, Jesus.* Scottlyn crossed the room and pulled out the chair on the other side of the table.

"You came. Thank you. What can I get you to drink?"

"That's not necessary—"

"No, I insist."

"OK. A white mocha cappuccino sounds good."

"I like those, too. I'll be right back."

Scottlyn remained at the table while the older woman

went to the counter and placed the order. She returned a few minutes later with a cup for both of them and two large chocolate chip cookies on a small tray. "I felt like a snack with our coffee. I hope you don't mind."

Both women sipped their drinks. Scottlyn tried to wait patiently, but it seemed as if Bradley's mom didn't know where to start.

Scottlyn broke off a piece of her cookie. "I'll admit to some curiosity about why you went to such trouble to track me down, Mrs. Nelson."

"Call me Penny, please."

Scottlyn nodded.

"I know that Gabe apologized for my behavior a few months ago, but I wanted to tell you how sorry I am in person. I had no right to treat you the way I did. I'm seeing a counselor. She's helped me see that I was way out of line." She lifted her shoulders in a small shrug. "I think between her and Gabe, and God, I'm about to get my balance back. Can you forgive me?"

"I forgave you months ago...Penny. I'm just glad that you're getting better." She patted her bag. "Thanks for the pictures. I'll put them away for Mercie. I know she'll treasure them when she's older."

Penny nodded. "Thanks for that." She studied Scottlyn in silence for a few seconds, finally leaning across the table. "Look, I know you don't have any reason to trust me, and I wouldn't blame you for laughing in my face at what I'm about to suggest, but I wondered if what Gabe said was true."

"What did he say?"

"That you might be open to us having a relationship with Mercie. A real grandparent relationship." She bolted ahead without giving Scottlyn a chance to answer. "The reason I'm asking is because Christmas is coming. I wouldn't think about asking for any time alone with her, not until we've had a chance to build some trust between us, but I wondered...would you like...I mean Gabe and I would love it if you and Mercie would..."

She trailed off as tears flooded her eyes.

"What I'm trying to say is that Gabe and I would love the chance to get to know you and Mercie better. We'd love it if you joined us for our Christmas Eve dinner."

"You want a relationship with both of us?"

Penny reached across the table and laid a hand across Scottlyn's. "More than anything else in the world. I'm not trying to replace my son. I'm not trying to weasel into your life for ulterior motives, but I think I'd be a good grandmother if I had the chance. And maybe we could learn to be friends." She pulled a napkin from the dispenser and blotted her eyes. "You don't have to answer me right now, but will you think about it?"

Scottlyn bit her lip. *Can I trust her, and even if the answer is yes, I have plans with Grant's family that night.*

Penny's shoulders slumped, obviously taking Scottlyn's hesitation as refusal. "I'm sorry, but I had to try." She reached for her bag and scooted her chair away from the table.

Scottlyn reached out a hand to stop her. "Don't go. I'm just trying to arrange my schedule in my head." *Not Christmas Eve and Christmas morning is out.* Her brows lifted as an idea took shape. *We could do snacks Christmas afternoon, at my house not theirs.* She'd be more comfortable with this meeting happening on her own turf with Grant and Diana both in attendance. *I shouldn't have a problem clearing it with Diana, and Grant...well he said these choices were mine.*

She looked into the hopeful eyes across the table and offered her alternative. "We'd love to have you, even Jared and Joel if they want to come." Scottlyn took a deep breath and faced the mother of the boy who'd raped her. "I think my baby should know all of her family. It was never my intention to have anyone begging for Mercie."

ALL ABOUT MERCIE

CHAPTER ONE

Scottlyn Rich should have listened to what her stomach tried to tell her that morning. She jolted to consciousness when the mattress convulsed around her, and giggles split the silence. Keeping her eyes closed for a second, she tried to capture the remnants of the dream that had troubled her sleep. Not really a nightmare, but—

"Mommy, wake up!"

Tiny hands framed Scottlyn's face, and a perfect rosebud mouth pressed a kiss to her lips. "You need to get up. We're getting weddinged today."

Scottlyn rolled to her side and tucked her three-year-old daughter close. She frowned and peered into tiny sky-blue eyes. "Weddinged?"

Mercie shook her head. "You told Gramma Diana that you had to get dressed for our wedding today 'cause Grant is marrying us."

"Silly girl." Scottlyn walked her fingers from the bottom of Mercies ribs to her collarbone, grinning when the child squirmed beneath the tickling. "We aren't getting *weddinged* today. I'm going to go look for our dresses, and you're spending the day with Grandma Penny."

Mercie's grin went to a scowl. "I want to marry Grant today."

Scottlyn pointed to the calendar on the wall across the room. The first five days in June were covered over with bright red Xs. "Just sixty-seven more days, if you'll go cross off today."

The three-year-old scrambled out of the bed. "Yay!"

Scottlyn moved a little slower, still unable to explain the uneasy feeling in the pit of her stomach that continued to prick at the edges of a much-anticipated day.

In the kitchen, Diana Kensington, surrogate mother and grandmother, flipped pancakes onto plates. Mercie pulled free of her mother's hand and ran to attach herself to Diana's leg.

"I get to marry Grant in just sixty-seben more days!"

Diana reached down and gave the child a quick hug. "He's a lucky guy. Hop into your chair, missy. Breakfast is ready."

Mercie raced to the table and climbed into the pub style chair like a monkey. Scottlyn shook her head. Her daughter had entered the world with all the aplomb of a freight train. She continued to have only two speeds, asleep or wired.

Diana brought the pancakes to the table with a bit more dignity while Scottlyn poured coffee and milk. "I wish I had that much energy."

"You and me both," Scottlyn said.

Diana sat and studied Scottlyn over her coffee cup. "You need energy? I thought you'd be bouncing off the walls today."

Scottlyn frowned. "I didn't sleep well."

"Bad dream?"

"Not that I can remember." She drizzled syrup onto Mercie's breakfast. "I can't put my finger on it. But I'm still a little twitchy."

Diana patted her hand. "You're shopping for your wedding dress today and having dinner with..." She paused, cutting her eyes to the little girl struggling to cut up a pancake. She reached across to help.

Mercie pushed Diana's hand away and flashed a syrupy smile. "I do it."

"Yes ma'am, miss independent." She looked back to Scottlyn. "You're shopping for your wedding dress and having dinner with your F.A.T.H.E.R. That's enough to twist anyone's stomach into knots."

"I guess." Scottlyn thought about the man who'd tossed her out of his home almost four years earlier when she'd refused to abort the baby planted in her by a rapist. They'd not spoken since before Mercie was born, until he'd called last week. She closed her eyes. *Father, please let this mean that he's ready for us to be a family again. I'd love for him to have a relationship with Mercie. You gave me Diana when I needed her most. I love her and I'm grateful, but I long to have Dad back in my life. If only I knew where my mother was...* Scottlyn allowed the prayer to trail off. *My mother?* Where did that come from?

"Scottlyn?"

Scottlyn jerked back to the present. "Sorry. I'm trying to be hopeful without getting my hopes up." She forked a bite of pancake and smeared it around in the syrup on her plate. "He sounded...different when we talked. If I knew for sure he'd called to make peace, I'd call him right now and offer to have lunch instead of dinner." She glanced at Mercie. "But I have to go slowly. I have more than just me to consider."

Diana sipped her coffee. "I hope he's come to his senses for your sake, but let's deal with first things first. You've been looking at dresses online and in magazines for months. Do you have any idea what you want?"

Scottlyn swallowed back the remains of her nerves. Diana was right. There was a lot on her plate today and taking one thing at a time was the best advice. "Not a clue, but between you, me, and Grant's mother, I'm sure we'll come up with something."

Nine discarded dresses later, the *something* she'd been so certain of still eluded her. She stepped out of the dressing room wearing number ten, arms held out to her sides, her bottom lip clenched in her teeth.

Diana and Melissa Weber, mother of the groom, both gasped.

"Wow," Diana said. "Simple but elegant."

Melissa moved her finger in a circular motion prompting Scottlyn to turn around.

Scottlyn obliged, trying to look in all of the mirrors at the same time. The dress left her arms bare and fell to the floor in drapes of sheer fabric that floated when she moved. The back featured a row of tiny buttons that marched up from her hips to the base of her neck. The front of the dress transitioned from a rounded neck to a fitted waist and fell to the floor in delicate waves.

"You look like a princess," Diana said.

"It's a gorgeous dress." The sales clerk nodded to a display of colorful scarves. It's designed to be belted to match the groom's cummerbund."

"What a wonderful way to accent," Melissa said.

"Do you like it?" Diana asked. "Because I think it's stunning."

Scottlyn relaxed her arms and smoothed her hands down the skirt. "It took the clerk twenty minutes to button me into it."

"Worth every second," Melissa told her. "Women only get to be a new bride once. Something so momentous should be a thoughtful and time consuming process."

Scottlyn faced the bank of mirrors a second time. She stood on her tiptoes, bundled up her long blonde hair, and imagined it clasped back with the combs that belonged to her mother. *It is beautiful.*

She remembered the price tag hanging on a hook in the fitting room and closed her eyes while her stomach sank. *Beautiful but hardly practical.* Surely there was something in this store just as lovely with a more attractive price tag.

She smiled at the clerk. "Thanks for your help. I don't mean to waste your time. But let's try the next one."

Diana took a few steps forward and cupped Scottlyn's chin in her hand. "You didn't answer my question. Do you like it?"

Scottlyn looked into the eyes of the woman who'd rescued her three-and-a-half years ago. The woman who'd made a home for her and her unborn child. The woman who'd become the mother she'd never had and a grandmother to Mercie. The woman who'd done way too much for her already.

The dress was perfect.

The dress was too much to ask for.

"This is an awesome dress. Grant and I have been saving for our wedding for two years. I have a generous dress budget, but this one is way over the limit."

Diana stared at Scottlyn before looking over her shoulder and addressing Melissa. "Did you hear anyone in this room mention money?"

"Nope," Melissa said.

"May I?" Diana asked.

"Be my guest." Melissa stepped to Diana's side and reached out to finger the sheer fabric.

Scottlyn frowned and looked from one woman to the other.

"Melissa and I have been saving as well." Diana began. "We knew that you and Grant planned to fund this wedding on your own. We think that's a great plan, and you've worked really hard, but—"

"I hope you don't think we're trying to meddle." Melissa twisted her hands at her waist.

"But," Diana continued. "We want you to have this dress, if it's the one you want."

Scottlyn studied the hopeful expressions of the two most important women in her life. *I can't let them...* "Thanks, you two, but Grant and I promised each other...

Diana held up a finger. "Melissa, I believe this is your cue."

Melissa dug deep into her bag, extracted her cell phone, and swiped the screen. She turned it to face Scottlyn and touched the play icon on the video. Grant's face popped to life, his dark eyes crinkled with laughter, his perfect mouth formed a wide grin.

"Hi, sweetheart. Buy the dress."

Melissa grinned. "We had a talk with Grant last night. We convinced him to let us help with this one thing. That's why we insisted that you try it on despite the price tag that you almost fainted over."

"We also videoed his answer so you'd believe us." Diana put her hands on Scottlyn's shoulders and turned her back to face the mirrors. "When you walk down the aisle in *sixty-seben* days, you'll be the most beautiful bride Sabor, Oklahoma, has ever seen. Grant's good with it. Will you let us help?"

Diana's mimicking of Mercie's excitement lightened the mood and drew a burst of laughter from Scottlyn. She wrapped an arm around each woman and hugged them to her sides. Before she could answer, a ringtone sounded from Scottlyn's purse in a chair across the room.

Melissa motioned with her head. "I'll bet that's my son now, calling to give you personal permission."

Scottlyn hiked up the skirt of the dress, stepped across

to the row of chairs, and pulled out her phone. She swiped it open without looking. "We found the perfect dress."

"Is this Scottlyn Rich?"

She blinked her eyes at the unfamiliar voice. "I'm sorry" She glanced at her screen, saw a number she didn't recognize, and lifted the phone to her ear again. "Yes, this is Scottlyn Rich."

"Ms. Rich, My name is Arnold Lewis. I'm calling from Bridge Park Hospital."

Scottlyn sank into the chair. The skirt rustled and billowed around her. *Mercie...Grant...* "What...?"

"I'm sorry to deliver this news over the phone, but your father's neighbor found him unconscious this morning. He was transported here by ambulance. We believe he's suffered an aneurysm."

The phone slipped from her fingers as the uneasiness in her stomach solidified into a cold block of panic. It hit the carpeted floor with a muffled thud. She left it there as she sprang up and tried to reach the row of tiny buttons on the back of the dress.

"Help me get out of this dress."

The older women hurried to her side. "Scottlyn, what...?"

The buttons eluded Scottlyn's trembling fingers. "Please. That was someone at Bridge Park Hospital. They just admitted Dad."

"Oh, sweetheart." Diana stepped behind her, and Scottlyn felt the older woman's fingers moving down the row of buttons. Melissa stepped away, her phone pressed to her ear. Hopefully Grant was on the other end.

Imprisoned by the dress, Scottlyn twisted her fingers at her waist and closed her eyes. *Jesus, please. Touch Daddy.* The moment she felt the dress sag from her shoulders,

Scottlyn gathered up the skirt and rushed back to the fitting room. When she came out a few minutes later, clad in jeans and a T-shirt, Diana and Melissa were waiting by the door with their bags.

"Did someone call Grant?"

"He'll meet us at Bridge Park." Melissa said.

Diana pressed Scottlyn's phone into her hand as they left the bridal shop behind. "Did they say what happened?"

Scottlyn slid into the back seat of Melissa's car. "A neighbor found him unconscious and called an ambulance, that's all I know." She looked up at Diana through a film of tears. "He has to be OK." She drew in a shuddering breath. "I should have called him this morning."

~ * ~

Grant took the chilled hands of his fiancé and tried to rub some warmth into them. "Tell me what you need me to do."

Scottlyn pulled one of her hands free and swiped at her nose. When she responded, her voice was no more than a despondent whisper. "I don't know."

Grant pulled her close and dropped a kiss on the crown of her head. His heart ached to see Scottlyn so lost and hurt. *Jesus, please comfort her right now. Please show me how to help her.*

Scottlyn turned into his chest. "I just wish...I wish I'd called him this morning when I thought about it. What if I could have been there for him when he needed someone? If I'd been there, maybe help would have reached him in time to save him."

Grant's lips flattened into a thin line. *Like he was there for you when you needed someone?* He bit back the thought. Instead, he shifted on the leather couch in the lobby of the funeral home and held her away from him so that he could look into her tear-stained blue eyes. "Sweetheart, there is always something we think we could have, would have, or should have done differently. Dwelling on those things right now will make you crazy." He shuffled through the feelings in his head and tried to dredge up something that would comfort and help. "Would you have been there if he'd asked you to be?"

Scottlyn nodded.

"Then that's what you need to hang on to. He asked to have dinner with you tonight, and you were willing to do that." He wiped a tear from her cheek with a thumb. "We don't get to see the future, babe." He pulled her close again. "That's God's job, and right now, we just have to trust that He has a plan." The words sounded lame coming out of his mouth, but it was the best he could do under the circumstances. The man hadn't done Scottlyn any favors. Father or not, other than concern over Scottlyn's obvious grief, Grant couldn't seem to work up any genuine sorrow over someone who'd yanked Scottlyn's world out from under her when she'd needed stability the most. Maybe, if Grant could distract her with the necessities, she'd get her feet under her.

"Did you call his lawyer? Right now you need access to insurance paperwork and the house." *Something she'd have if the man had been the father she deserved.* Grant swallowed the thought and willed the negative aside. Some of that was going to spill past his lips if he wasn't careful. He wanted to help Scottlyn, not cause her more pain.

Scottlyn's breath shuddered against his chest. "I left a message with the lawyer's secretary. Harold Cole is an old family friend. I know he'll get back with us as soon as he can."

She sat up, and Grant followed her gaze to a somber man dressed in black seated at the desk in the next room. "The staff has been so kind, I just...I don't know what to do until I talk to Mr. Cole."

As if conjured by Scottlyn's words, the outside door opened, and a short, balding man sporting a handlebar moustache and wearing a dark suit stepped through. He looked around, spotted Scottlyn, and hurried in their direction.

Scottlyn scrambled from the couch and met him halfway. The man put his hands on her shoulders and whispered something Grant couldn't hear before pulling Scottlyn into his arms for a quick embrace. When he stepped away, Scottlyn caught his hand and led him to the couch.

"Mr. Cole, I want you to meet Grant Weber, my fiancé. Grant, this is Daddy's lawyer, Harold Cole."

The portly older gentleman held out a hand. "Good to meet you." He studied Grant with shrewd brown eyes. "You're Brent Weber's son, aren't you?"

Grant returned the handshake. "Yes, sir. You know my dad?"

"Sabor's law community is a small pool, young man. Your father and I have been legal opponents as well as allies more than once over the years. He's a good man. Please give him my regards."

Grant nodded.

"Well." The lawyer turned his attention back to Scottlyn. "This is an unexpected and sorry business. I know you have questions. Tell me how I can help."

Scottlyn sat down and motioned to the chair next to the sofa. "I guess you know about the...problems between me and my dad?"

The older man nodded.

Scottlyn tilted her head at the gentleman still seated at the desk in the next room. "I don't know how to answer any of their questions. They need information about Dad's life insurance policy. Did he have burial arrangements made someplace? The hospital is looking for health insurance info. I need..."

Her voice broke, and Grant took her hand.

"I need to get a suit out of his closet. The next door neighbor locked the door behind the EMTs this morning, and I know Daddy changed the locks on the house right after..." Scottlyn leaned forward and put her face in her hands. "This wasn't supposed to happen. We were scheduled to have dinner tonight. I hoped he'd forgiven me..."

The lawyer leaned forward and stopped Scottlyn's flow of words with a hand on her knee. "Forgiven you? Dear child, it was your father who needed forgiveness."

Grant raised his eyebrows. He couldn't speak the truth to Scottlyn, but maybe Harold Cole could.

Scottlyn raised her head, and the old lawyer continued. "Your father was my friend since before you were born, but I never agreed with the way he handled the...your...situation. There is nothing I can say to make it better, but I can say that your mother's desertion made William Rich bitter in ways even he didn't even understand. Your father was a man of deep feelings. He never quite got over losing Jocelyn. I can't believe he pushed you and his grandchild out of his life but never divorced the woman who left you both behind without a word."

"Wait a minute." Grant frowned. "They're still married...after all these years?"

Harold nodded. "I drew up divorce papers a dozen

times over the years. William refused to sign them every time. Deep down, I think he hoped she'd come back to him. I never understood it."

He sat back. "Now, on to business. As for insurance, I have copies of your father's health and life insurance policies at the office. I'll forward those to the appropriate parties first thing in the morning. Rest easy, he had more than enough to give him a proper send off." He slipped a hand in his pocket and pulled out a key ring with two keys. He held them out to Scottlyn. "This is a key to the house and one to his safe deposit box. The house is yours now to do with as you please—"

"How...? I thought..."

The lawyer looked from Scottlyn to Grant and back. "Scottlyn, you are his sole heir and beneficiary. Despite his rash actions, I know your father loved you very much. Just like he could never sign divorce papers, he never revised his will. The mortgage is paid, and in your mother's continued absence, the house belongs to you."

CHAPTER TWO

"Jocelyn Rich, Jocelyn Rich, Jocelyn Rich." The woman dabbed concealer under her eyes and continued to mutter the name she hadn't spoken in over a decade. She needed to get used to the sound of it, to answering to it. She studied the two pictures wedged into the upper right corner of the mirror. Mother and daughter—long blonde hair, clear blue eyes. The mother's eyes held just a touch of something innocent and trusting. She snickered into the mirror. "Lost that, didn't you?"

She took a step back and shook out her new haircut, satisfied that her reflection came as close to the picture as she was likely to get, considering that more than seventeen years separated then and now. There wasn't much hope that Scottlyn would recognize her either way, but if there were old pictures floating around, she wanted the resemblance to be obvious.

William's funeral was later today. She would have missed this opportunity if not for Andrew's quick thinking. Her boyfriend had rushed home on Wednesday with the paper open to William Rich's obituary. Forty-eight hours hadn't given them much time to prepare, but sometimes life threw you a curve ball. With Andrew's help, she intended to smash this one out of the park.

She situated a new black hat on her head, pulled the netting over her eyes, and nodded into the mirror. "You'll do."

She strutted into the cramped living room of the ancient apartment and struck a pose in the doorway.

Andrew looked up from the television. His gaze started at the floor and traveled from her shiny new shoes to the fresh highlights in her hair. His wolf whistle drowned out the commercial playing on the tube.

"Oh, baby! You look good enough to eat. I know I balked at the expense, but those shoes were a hundred dollars well spent." He patted his lap and wiggled his eyebrows. "Come over here and sit on Daddy's lap for a second."

She grinned. "Not normally an invitation I'd resist, but I need to get on the road."

He nodded, rose from his seat, and sauntered to where she stood. He studied the finished product in more detail.

"What do you think?"

"If there's an afterlife, you'll have old William begging to come back." He dropped a kiss onto her mouth. "Do you think you'll be home tonight?"

She shrugged. "Depends on how it goes. You've got the night shift again, right?"

He nodded.

"OK. If I'm not here when you get home, I'll call you first thing in the morning. Wish me luck."

"You aren't going to need it."

Bolstered by Andrew's confidence, she left the apartment without a backward glance. She didn't plan to attend the funeral, but she would put in an appearance at the house, offer what comfort she could to Scottlyn, and in the process, maybe...just maybe, the girl could be convinced to share part of Daddy's estate with a long lost, grieving widow and mother.

Scottlyn fingered her black skirt. The cotton was cool beneath her fingers, but it would wilt quickly in the June heat. *That's OK, it will be in good company with my heart.* How was it possible for life to change so abruptly in three days? On Tuesday, she been trying on white lace, today she wore black. On Tuesday, she'd hoped that her father might give her away at her wedding, today her father was being buried. On Tuesday, her heart had been happy despite a niggle of misgiving, today she understood what those reservations had been about. She stared into the past and the might have beens of the future, unable to stop the tears that streamed down her face. Today, the dream of ever again hearing her father say I *love you* became a fairy tale. *Oh, Daddy.*

"Mommy, why are you sad? Do you have a boo-boo?"

She blinked and used a crumpled tissue to dab at her eyes. Mercie stood in the doorway of Scottlyn's bedroom, a look of concern scrunching up her little face. How could Scottlyn answer? Her baby had no point of reference where her grandfather Rich was concerned. She'd never met him. *Now she never will.* The thought ignited fresh tears as she sat. "Come here, baby." She pulled Mercie into her lap, and held her close.

"Sometimes grownups get sad. It makes their heart hurt." She brushed back Mercie's long blonde hair. "Are you ready to go visit with Grandma and Grandpa?"

Mercie nodded. "They said we could go to the zoo and feed the bears." Mercie leaned back and formed her small hands into claws and pawed at Scottlyn's shirt. "Grrrr." Her smile was impish. "They like marshmallows."

"Almost as much as you."

The doorbell rang, and Mercie scrambled out of Scottlyn's lap. "They're here!" Mercie ran for the entryway, leaving Scottlyn to follow several steps behind.

Baby, her teacup poodle, got there first. Child and dog stood by the door, one yapping, one clapping, and both bouncing with excitement. The sight lightened Scottlyn's mood and had a smile tugging at her lips. The combination of toddler and dog was often daunting, but it was impossible to remain sad in the face of their exuberance. *Jesus, thank You. Even when my heart is broken, I'm blessed. Please help me to hold onto that.*

Scottlyn pulled the door open, and before she could speak, she found herself engulfed in the arms of Penny Nelson. "Sweetheart, Gabe and I are so sorry. Is there anything we can do?"

Scottlyn returned the hug and looked at Gabe over Penny's shoulder. She stepped back and forced a smile for Mercie's sake. "You're doing it, and I've been so busy, I haven't even had a chance to thank you." She sniffed. "Mercie duty three days in a row. I—"

"Pleasure, not duty," Gabe corrected her. He stepped around his wife, swooped Mercie into his arms, and turned her in a wide circle. "What are grandparents for?"

Mercie wrapped her arms around his neck and placed a loud kiss on his mouth. "Did you bring the marshmallows?"

"Three bags. Think that'll be enough?"

Mercie nodded, her blue eyes bright with excitement. "Do efelants eat marshmallows too?"

The picture tore at Scottlyn's heart. *I won't cry...I won't cry...I refuse to cry.* "You guys are the best. I'm so glad you decided to be part of my baby's life."

"And that's enough of that," Penny told her. "You take care of...what you need to do today, and we'll have Mercie home right after breakfast tomorrow morning." She turned to her husband and grandchild. "You guys ready?"

"I think you forgot something." Diana stepped into

the doorway. She held out Mercie's backpack and stuffed monkey. "Can't leave without your things."

Penny took them. "Yep, we'd be looking for those later." She handed the monkey to Mercie. "The bears are waiting. Tell Mom and Grandma Diana bye."

Mercie waved, dissolving in giggles when Gabe swung her up onto his shoulders and galloped to the car with a monkey perched on his head.

Scottlyn watched with tears in her eyes. Diana put an arm around her shoulders. The gentle touch was her undoing. "Why couldn't that have been Daddy?" She turned into the arms of the only mother she'd ever known and wept for things that would never be.

CHAPTER THREE

Her father's house was overrun with well-intentioned people. They chatted in small clumps. Some helped themselves to the smorgasbord of food laid out in the kitchen. Each one offered Scottlyn a word of support or shared a story about her father. The attention was stifling.

Scottlyn moved from room to room in the house she'd grown up in. Other than a brief visit two days ago to retrieve burial clothes for her father, she hadn't been inside in more than three years. *It belongs to me now.* The reality hadn't sunk in yet. So she wandered and took comfort in the familiarity. But the uneasiness that had filled her a few days ago returned, etching itself deeper in her mind with every breath. A funeral today, her father's estate to deal with, wedding plans to finish. *Jesus, I need You to hold me up.*

She paused in the doorway of her old room. Not a scrap of her presence remained. Daddy had emptied her out of this room like he'd emptied her out of his heart. She imagined him in there, angrily boxing up her things, removing any trace that he'd ever had a daughter. *Daddy, will I ever know why?*

Bitterness squeezed her heart in a relentless grip. Abortion or adoption had been the only options he'd accept after the rape that left her pregnant. Scottlyn refused both. For that grand disobedience, he'd ordered her out of the house and out of his life. She'd walked out with a bag of clothes, her school books, an iPod, and the combs her mother had worn in her hair on her wedding day.

She closed her eyes and leaned against the doorjamb. *God, I know I made the right choice where Mercie is concerned. You've been there for me every step of the way. I always hoped...* The prayer went on hold when her fingers encountered a series of indentions carved into the wood she rested against. Scottlyn bent to examine them. "Measurements." Someone had painted over the numbers, but the grooves were still there. She stooped and walked her fingers up the marks, fifteen in all. A tradition carried out on each birthday from when she first learned to stand on her own until she reached her full growth. *Daddy said Mom started it, but he always made such a big deal out of it. Pocketknife, ruler, and a marker. Most parents just made a mark of some sort. Daddy carved me into the wood of the house.* Scottlyn's lips inched up in a smile. *Maybe he did love me, just a little.*

Her smile bloomed in force when Grant's arms slid around her waist. She leaned against him and breathed deep of the spicy cologne he favored.

"What you got there?" he asked.

"Proof that my father loved me." She turned in his arms and snuggled close. "I've been walking through the house, looking for some remnant of my presence. Something I could hold onto that was just mine and Daddy's."

The arms around her tightened. "Baby, you've got to get past this. The man was a shortsighted idiot who didn't care for anyone but himself—"

"What?" Scottlyn shoved out of his arms and put her hands on her hips.

Grant took a step back. He ran both hands through

his hair before meeting Scottlyn's glare. "Scottie, I'm sorry. I just...I mean..." He took a deep breath. "Seeing you so hurt is killing me, OK? I shouldn't have said what I just said. I've been asking God for strength to keep my thoughts to myself, but that one slipped out."

She leaned into his space, her words a whispered hiss. "You just called my father, the father I just buried, an idiot."

He put his hands on her shoulders, ran them down her arms, and brought her fingers to a place over his heart. "I'm the idiot. I have opinions about what happened between you and him, but I should keep them to myself." He raised her hands and brushed her knuckles with a kiss. "Scottie, I love you. That automatically makes anyone who hurts you the bad guy." He squeezed her hands. "Forgive me?"

Scottlyn studied his expression. "I guess I get that. I've been struggling with some of the same feelings." She waved at the marks in the doorjamb. "One minute looking for some clue that I was loved, the next wondering why I should care either way." She freed her hands, placed them on his shoulders, and raised to her tiptoes to place a kiss on his mouth. "So, yes, I forgive you, but I need you to let me work these feelings out for myself."

She leaned against him and rested her forehead on his chest. "I just feel so disjointed."

"How do you mean?"

"Alone. Unanchored. Mom's gone, Daddy's dead...I'm an orphan."

"Scottie..."

"I know how pitiful and extreme that sounds, but I want to be honest with you, so you can understand where I'm coming from." She paused and tried to put her thoughts into words that sounded a little less pathetic. She wanted his support, not his sympathy.

"It's hard to explain. I know you love me, and I know Diana loves me, but it's not the love of a parent. How many adopted kids grow up loved by parents who *chose* to love them and spend their lives looking for the people who gave them birth? No matter how old we are, no matter how much we're loved, I don't think we ever outgrow the need for that connection. It's an internal part of who we are, at least it is for me."

Scottlyn raised her head. "Mom's been gone for so long, I can't remember what she looked like. She isn't coming back. I accepted that a long time ago. But Daddy? Despite everything that happened, I had this place in my heart that hoped love would win in the end, and he'd want me back in his life. It's going to take me a while to adjust to the fact that I've lost them both."

~ * ~

The ancient Chevy sputtered to a stop at the curb in front of William's house. She turned off the engine, and the infernal machine rattled and coughed for thirty seconds before it died, filling the air with an acrid stench. Her eyes closed in frustration. A new car moved to number three on her wish list—just beneath *get as much of William's money as she could and leave Sabor, Oklahoma, behind for good.*

She climbed out of the car, slammed the door, and gave the crowd of surrounding vehicles a dismissive sneer. Seemed like the man was more popular in death than he'd ever been in life. She pulled a compact out of her bag and checked her hair and makeup. *Showtime.*

The tears she needed came easily enough. So what if

they were tears of joyful anticipation? Her ship was about to sail with her at the helm, and that was enough to make any woman weep. From the outside, they would be indistinguishable from sorrow.

As she navigated the walk, she allowed her shoulders to slump, her head to hang. She sidled through the front door, wringing her hands at her waist and twisting a plain gold band on the ring finger of her left hand. She clung to the sides of the room, avoiding the press of strangers. *Sabor's upper crust.* She scoffed. Nothing but small town losers, using William's death as a chance to strut their best Walmart wardrobes. Jocelyn ignored them all. There were only two people she needed to see, Scottlyn and the lawyer. She figured they would spot her soon enough.

While she waited she appraised her surroundings. *Used furniture doesn't bring a lot, but I could get an easy hundred for that sofa and another twenty-five for the chair.* Her eyes studied the outdated electronics, and she shook her head in derision. *The man was a dinosaur.* This was probably the last house in Sabor without a flat screen TV, and the computer equipment on the desk in the corner was just as obsolete.

She meandered through the crowd of mourners. The electronics might be out-of-date, but the house was full of expensive, easily pawned items that made her fingers itch with the desire to examine and pocket. She resisted the temptation. Scottlyn was her primary target today. It was imperative that she win the girl's sympathy. If she could accomplish that—and her story was a good one, if she did say so herself—everything else would fall into place. The days ahead would provide plenty of opportunity for her sticky fingers.

For now, she did her best to blend in, speaking to no one, offering a small grief stricken smile to anyone who caught her eye. She helped herself to a plate of goodies and something to drink. Her eyes lingered over the selection of sodas, tea, and lemonade lined up on the kitchen cabinet, searching for something stronger before settling for iced tea. *Who throws a wake with no booze?*

All the while, she kept an eye out for Scottlyn or the lawyer. She needed to establish her return in front of witnesses, needed an opportunity to finagle her way into the good graces of Scottlyn and that old family lawyer. They had to be here somewhere.

She moved back to the living room just as a trio of individuals entered from the other end of the house. *There they are.* She scrutinized her prey from a comfortable distance. She'd only seen Harold Cole one time, and he'd aged badly. His belly hung over his belt, and that ridiculous mustache did nothing to hide the additional lines on his face. Scottlyn, on the other hand, had grown into a beautiful young lady. Jocelyn searched her heart for any feelings of connection and came up empty. *I'll need to be careful there. Indifference won't get me what I want.*

She put the plate aside, primed her tears, and made her move. She stumbled across the room and threw herself into Harold Cole's arms.

The surprised lawyer sputtered and tried to disentangle himself. "What are you doing?"

"Oh, Harold. How did this happen?"

Harold grabbed her upper arms and held her at arm's length. He stared into her face. She knew the instant he recognized her.

"Jocelyn?"

She nodded.

"You have a lot of nerve showing your face here."

Next to him Scottlyn studied her with a frown. "Jocelyn...?" She tilted her head. "Mom?"

CHAPTER FOUR

"Oh baby, look at you."

Scottlyn blinked back tears as the woman's hands cupped her chin and turned her head from side to side.

"You grew up without me. You're so beautiful."

The words were a warm balm over Scottlyn's troubled heart. "Mom?"

"It's me baby."

Scottlyn allowed herself to be pulled into an embrace.

"I'm here, and I'm never going away again."

Harold Cole harrumphed. "We need to take this tender reunion out of the doorway and away from the public." He motioned to a closed door. "Grant, see if anyone is in the den."

Grant stepped away, looked inside, and waved them forward. "It's empty."

Scottlyn trailed behind the group, unable to take her eyes off her mother. She watched her every move, seriously afraid that if she so much as blinked, the woman might disappear again. *I'm not alone. Thank You, Jesus!* In the annals of answered prayers, this had to be a record. She allowed Grant to lead her to a seat. He took a position behind her, his hands resting lightly on her shoulders.

Jocelyn...*Mom*...took the loveseat while Harold closed the door and leaned against it. Maybe he, too, was afraid she'd vanish. Scottlyn's estimation of the situation changed when the lawyer crossed his arms and nailed her mother with a cold stare.

"What are you doing here?"

She blinked. "I came to see my daughter." The brightness of tears filled her eyes. "I came to say good-bye to the only man I ever loved."

Harold's snort bordered on rude. "Love? You don't know the meaning of the word. I'm surprised God doesn't strike you where you sit. You walked out the front door of this house seventeen years ago and never looked back. It's a little late to claim *love* now."

Her long-lost mother wrung her hands in her lap, meeting the irate lawyer's gaze head on. "But I can explain. None of that was my fault."

"You—"

"Stop!" Scottlyn rubbed at her temples. "I just buried my father. I don't need an argument piled on top of that." She frowned at the lawyer. "Is this woman my mother?"

Harold nodded.

"Then let her talk." The tears pressing Scottlyn's eyes for the last five minutes overflowed. "I have a right to hear what she has to say."

His brows gathered low over his eyes, but he made a gesture for her mother to continue.

Scottlyn tilted her head at the smug look that flitted across Jocelyn's face. Her moment of uneasiness melted away the second her mom's gaze came back to hers. *Our eyes are so identical...the way she holds her head. It's like looking in a mirror.*

"Thank you, sweetheart. I have so much to tell you, and it's difficult enough without arguments."

Scottlyn closed her eyes and listened to her mother's voice. She had no memories from when her mother had left. She'd only been eighteen months old. If she concentrated, maybe her voice would spark a memory.

"Scottlyn."

Her eyes snapped open.

"Baby, look at me. You're the only one in this room who deserves an explanation. There's no way to bring back the years we've lost, but I think I can explain, if you're willing to hear me out."

Scottlyn didn't trust her voice.

She simply nodded.

~ * ~

Jocelyn smiled and hoped that it appeared less predatory than it felt. *Kid's so desperate, I could tell her I'd been asleep in a castle, waiting for Prince Charming's kiss, and she'd lap it up.* Good news was that she was too young to remember anything that actually happened. She leaned forward, her eyes steady on Scottlyn's face.

"You were the best thing that ever happened to me. The day you were born, the first time I held you, I knew what my life was all about." Some of the tension between her shoulders relaxed as the story flowed exactly as she'd rehearsed. The rapt expression on Scottlyn's face didn't hurt either. "You have a baby. You know how that is?"

Scottlyn smiled. "I do. Mercie changed my life in ways I never imagined. I can't wait for you to meet her."

A kid to impress, oh joy! "I can't believe I'm a grandma."

"Can we move this along?" The disgruntled question came from the lawyer still leaning against the door.

Jocelyn spared him a quick glance. *Uncomplicate my life and drop dead, would you?* She directed her words to Scottlyn. "I need to tell the whole story for you to understand what happened."

Scottlyn pressed her lips together and glanced at the lawyer. "Harold, please?"

The old lawyer threw his hands up in obvious disgust. "Whatever."

"Anyway," Jocelyn continued, "you were the light of my life. But, as much as I loved you, that first year was one of the most difficult I'd ever experienced. I know now that I was a victim of severe postpartum depression. I couldn't shake it. William couldn't understand that it was my hormones making me crazy, not you." She forced an anguished sigh into the room. "I had to take a break or lose my mind."

"Oh, Mom."

"I know...it was a selfish decision, but I convinced myself that I was weighing the long-term benefits against the pain of a short-term separation. I only intended to be gone a few days...a week at the most, and you would never remember."

"Then why did you stay gone?" Scottlyn crossed her arms and turned slightly away.

Jocelyn recognized agitation in Scottlyn's posture. Jocelyn hadn't lost her, but she needed to tread carefully. She needed the girl's sympathy back in her court sooner rather than later.

"I got tossed into a stinking Mexican jail and sentenced to seventeen years for drug trafficking."

"What?"

The question came from the young man standing behind Scottlyn. *Boyfriend?* Jocelyn studied him and his incredulous expression. He wasn't buying her story. How much influence did he have over Scottlyn? She caught a glint of light and focused on the engagement ring on Scottlyn's left hand. *Ahh...*"And you are...?"

"I'm sorry, Mom, I should have introduced you right

away." Scottlyn turned to smile up at the young man. "This is my fiancé, Grant Weber. Someone else you'll need to get to know."

Careful...flies and honey. She pasted a smile on her face. "Grant, thank you."

Grant's brows rose, lines of confusion etched around his eyes. "For...?"

"For being here for my baby this week. It's obvious that you love her very much. I'm so glad Scottlyn has someone strong to lean on right now."

"Hmm." His gaze bored into hers as if determined to pick through her thoughts. "You're welcome. Jail?"

His abrupt response flustered her. A bead of sweat traced a path between her breasts, and she fidgeted at the sensation. She risked a second glance at his stony countenance and hurried back to her story. "When I left here, I flew to Cozumel. I took long walks on the beach. Watched the sunset."

Scottlyn cocked her head at the words. "Sounds like you had a good time." The sarcasm in her words was unmistakable.

"Baby, I'm sorry if parts of my story hurt. I owe you honesty."

She shook free of Grant's hands and stood to stare down at Jocelyn. "Did Daddy know where you went?"

Jocelyn shook her head. "He never would have let me go. He took you to the park for a Saturday picnic. I made sure I was gone before you got home."

"No note, no explanation, no goodbyes? Just"—she snapped her fingers—"poof, you were gone?"

"I know how selfish it must sound." Her eyes filled with fresh tears. "But I missed you every day."

Scottlyn's hand shook when she ran it through her hair. Jocelyn heard her mutter, "Few days."

She sat back down. "OK, so you only planned to be gone for a few days. What happened?"

Jocelyn took a deep breath and prepared to launch into the meat of her story. "I was betrayed."

She looked around the room. Three sets of eyes looked back, each shining with a different emotion. Disapproval from the lawyer, distrust from the fiancé, but in Scottlyn's eyes she saw a spark of hope. Jocelyn focused on the one who needed to believe her. "While I was at the resort, I met another woman. Her name was Lizzie. We were close to the same age and both traveling alone, so we hung out a little bit, did some sightseeing together. She's the one who told me about the postpartum thing. Her sister suffered from it. Knowing my problem had a name and a cure gave me such hope. I knew things would be better once I got home." She cleared her throat, waiting for some response. She continued when her audience remained silent.

"Anyway, we were booked on the same flight back to the States. We went to the airport together, and when it came time for me to board the plane, they found cocaine in my bag."

"Oh, dear Lord!" The lawyer finally left his place at the door to stride around the room. He ran a hand across his baldhead. "You tried to smuggle drugs into the country?"

"No, Harold. I promise. It wasn't me. It was Lizzie!"

Harold glared. "How...?"

"I don't know. The only time that bag was out of my sight was when I went to the restroom. It was crowded, and I asked Lizzie to watch it for me. The next thing I knew, I was being carted out of the airport in handcuffs. It had to be her."

The story flowed faster as Jocelyn warmed to her subject. "They took me to jail, confiscated all my luggage and paperwork, and sentenced me to seventeen years."

Grant leaned forward. "And in seventeen years, you never found the chance to let someone know where you were?'

She nodded and allowed her expression to harden. "You people have no idea. A Mexican prison isn't like an American one. You don't get a phone call. There are no privileges, at least not in the hole I was in. Three barely edible meals a day, a cot with a one-inch mattress, and ten hours of labor a day." Jocelyn smudged a tear from under her eye.

"I just got out a month ago. I didn't have a driver's license or my birth certificate, much less a passport—"

Grant shook his head. "You could have called—"

"Hi, you don't know me, but this is Jocelyn Rich. I'm stranded in Mexico, and I need your help to get home." She shook her head. "Sounds like an email scheme I've heard about. I went straight to the embassy to see what I needed to do to get home. It took three weeks to get everything in order. I got back a week ago, and I was looking for a way to reach out to my husband and daughter. I wanted a chance to know the woman my daughter had become. I wanted to tell William that I was sorry." She bent forward and put her face in her hands. Her voice rose in a howl of grief. "And now, I'll never get that chance."

~ * ~

"Oh, Mom." Scottlyn left her seat and knelt on the floor in front of Jocelyn. She wrapped the woman in her arms and rocked. "Don't cry. It's OK. We'll figure this out together."

Grant frowned as his fiancé and a stranger bonded

over their grief. He looked over at Harold, caught the lawyer's nod toward the door, and followed the older man out.

With the door shut behind them, Harold looked Grant in the eye. "Did you buy any of that?"

"Not a single word," Grant assured him. "I was raised by one of the best lawyers in this part of the country. I learned to read body language while I studied my ABCs."

Harold nodded.

"You're sure this woman is Scottlyn's mother?"

Harold's stare threatened to bore a hole through the wood of the door. "I knew her back then. I'd have to say yes. But the story she just told." He shook his head. "She's lying."

"Agreed. If she's only been back a week, how did she know Scottlyn has a daughter? And that thing with the email scheme? If you've been locked away for fifteen years, where would you see that? I'm no judge, but she looks pretty healthy for someone so starved and overworked."

"Exactly." Harold picked at his bottom lip. "Knowing she's lying and proving it are two different things. Her story can be checked out, but it'll take some time."

Grant's answer was a whispered groan. "And proving to my fiancée that the woman who claims to be her mother is a liar?" *Oh, Scottie.* "That's a tightrope I'm not looking forward to walking."

CHAPTER FIVE

The grandfather clock's seven chimes matched the throbbing in Scottlyn's head as the last of her father's friends departed. The only people remaining in the house were Grant, Mr. Cole...and her mom. Scottlyn closed the front door and rested her forehead against the polished wood. After the stress of the last two days and the funeral this morning, the day-long parade of visitors, and the unexpected appearance of her mother, her emotions were walking a thin line between exhaustion and overload.

Scottlyn drew in a deep breath. *I want to spend some time with Mom, but I'm so tired.* She turned and found her mother seated on the living room sofa, legs crossed, foot swinging idly, her gaze roaming the empty room as if looking for something...or someone. *I know the feeling.* Maybe she wasn't the only one who could use some quiet time this evening to wrap her head around everything that had happened today. Tomorrow was Saturday and probably the best option for a lengthy reunion. They could get together after Mercie came home and spend the whole day getting reacquainted.

She crossed the room and sat on the other end of the sofa. "Mom..." She stumbled over the unfamiliar word, cleared her throat, and started over. "Mom, what are your plans for the next couple of days?"

Her mother's breath hitched and her shoulders

slumped. "I'll go back to Tulsa, I guess."

Scottlyn frowned at the despair she heard in her mother's voice. "Tulsa?"

She nodded. Blonde hair covered her features like a curtain when she bowed her head over the hands she held clasped in her lap. "I have some old friends there. Once I made it back to the states, I called them. They understood my need to be as close to you and William as I could while I tried to find the best way to contact you. They're helping me...financially...until I can get back on my feet." When she continued, her voice had dwindled to a whisper. "They helped me get my license, loaned me a car, and gave me some gas money."

Her eyes were bright with tears when she looked up. "I'd love to stay a few days, but I don't have any money..."

Scottlyn caught her bottom lip in her teeth. There was no way she could send this woman away before they had a chance to talk. She looked up to the ceiling. Surely Grant would understand that. She scooted across the cushions and took her mother's hand in hers. "If I can make arrangements for you, can you call your friends and see if they can do without the car for a couple of days?"

"What kind of arrangements?"

"I think I can come up with the money to get you in to a nice hotel for the weekend—"

"Absolutely not." Her mother jerked her hand free. "I didn't come back here to sponge off of my baby girl."

Scottlyn met her mother's indignant stare. "It's not *sponging* if I offer. Please?" She heard the whine in her voice and didn't care. "I can't let you walk back out of my life without getting to know you first. A couple of days isn't a lot of time, but it's better than nothing."

Her mother's lips trembled when she smiled. "You

grew up with a generous heart. If you're sure, I'll give them a call. If they can spare the car, I'd love to stay for the weekend, if that's what you want."

Scottlyn sighed in relief. "Sit right here. Let me go talk to Grant."

~ * ~

Jocelyn watched her walk away. That had been way too easy. It was scary to think there were such gullible people in the world. Even more scary to think that someone so easily deceived could be related to her. *Didn't you teach her anything about the real world, William?*

She settled back in the cushions. She'd let the girl have a few days of wish fulfillment and be on her way just as soon as she could get her hands on some serious cash.

She replayed their conversation in her head. She hadn't said anything that would lead them anywhere if they decided to check. The name Jocelyn Rich wasn't on anything current except the DMV records for the license she'd applied for yesterday, and if they found that, it would only verify her story.

Jocelyn crossed her arms and waited. As far as she was concerned, it was a downhill coast from here.

Grant put a cup of fresh coffee on the kitchen table in front of the lawyer. He sat, but bounced back up when Scottlyn entered the room. He crossed to her with his arms outstretched. "Scottie, you look so worn out. Is everyone gone?"

"Everyone except Mother."

"Well, find out where she's staying. You guys can get some rest tonight and catch up all you want tomorrow."

Scottlyn rose to her tiptoes and brushed a kiss across

his lips. "How come you're always a step ahead of me? That's exactly what I came in here to talk to you about." She stepped out of his arms, opened the refrigerator, and emerged with a can of soda. She popped the top and leaned against the counter. "Mother needs a place to stay for the weekend."

Grant studied her but held his peace while Scottlyn related the recent conversation with her mother. *I know where this is going.* Maybe the thought was petty, but the woman's story hadn't impressed him. There was something evil about Jocelyn Rich, and every protective instinct he had was on high alert. *Father, please give me some direction here. This situation could drive a wedge between Scottlyn and me that we can never overcome.*

Scottlyn finished and took a deep breath. "I need to take some money out of our wedding fund."

"Scottie..."

Scottlyn put her hands on her hips. "What?"

"We promised each other not to touch that money."

"I know that, but don't you think this situation trumps that promise? You know I wouldn't ask if there were another way."

Grant closed his eyes and considered the fifteen thousand dollars they'd worked and scrimped for two years to save. Certainly not a fortune, but a lot for two college students. Money intended to fund their wedding, honeymoon, and the expenses of getting into their first apartment. "How much?"

"A thousand?"

Grant stared at her.

"I know it sounds like a lot, but it really isn't." She put her soda aside and held out her hand.

Grant took it and she pulled his arm around her. He closed his eyes when she nestled close. It wasn't about the money, not entirely. *She has to know I'd give her the moon if I could.* He wrapped her tighter, more worried about the possibility of her broken heart than a broken bank account.

"It's my mother, Grant, someone I'd given up all hope of ever knowing. Do you remember what I said earlier about feeling like an orphan?"

"Yes, I..."

She stopped him with a finger on his lips. "It's gone. I know you thought I was a little crazy when I said it, and I know you probably think I've lost my mind now, but it's like God heard me before I ever prayed and gave me the one thing I needed. There's a Bible verse like that somewhere, isn't there?"

"Isaiah 65:24." Harold Cole's words drew their attention, reminded them of his presence. "And it shall come to pass before they call, I will answer; and while they are yet speaking, I shall hear." He shrugged. "I've taught the adult Sunday school class at my church for twenty years." He focused on Scottlyn. "I know this feels like an answer to your prayers, but I have to advise you towards a little caution. You don't know anything about this woman."

Grant rubbed her back when she stiffened in his arms.

The lawyer continued before Scottlyn could voice her objections. "But she's your mother. We both"—he motioned between himself and Grant—"understand that. Why don't you tell us what you had in mind?"

"I want to keep her close for a few days, and when it comes to hotels in Sabor, there are two choices, cheap and run down here in town, or nice but expensive on the interstate. So, two or three hundred for the nice hotel for a few nights, and money for meals and gas. I'm sure she didn't pack a suitcase before she came to town today, so we need to make a trip to the store..."

"Scottie..."

"I might have a better option." Harold spoke again before the discussion could become their first financial disagreement. "She could stay here. The house belongs to her, after all."

Scottlyn tilted her head. "I thought you said—not that I care, but—didn't you say the house was mine?"

The lawyer nodded. "Yes, I did, the house and the proceeds of your father's estate, which should be sizable. But that's no longer relevant." He pulled his hands down his face. "Remember I said your father had neither divorced your mother nor changed his will?"

Scottlyn nodded.

"When I told you that your father's estate would come to you, I was working under the assumption that Jocelyn Rich was history." He raised his hands in a motion of surrender. "Your father looked for her for several years. When nothing turned up, when years passed without a word, I think we both assumed she was dead. I would have suggested having her declared so, but I knew your father would never agree." He scooted away from the table, crossed to the sink, and emptied his cup. "I haven't looked at your father's will in years, but if memory serves, the house and as well as half of William's assets will fall to her."

The old family friend pinned Scottlyn with a no nonsense stare. "I know this won't win me any points, but her appearance today is more than a little suspicious."

"But she explained..."

"Yes, she did," Harold said, "but Bible verses and answered prayers aside, there are holes in her story big enough to drive a truck through. I'd be doing you and your father's estate an injustice if I didn't initiate an investigation into her claims. In the meantime, she is within her rights to stay here if she chooses. The house is certainly more comfortable than any hotel, the pantry is well stocked, and she won't need much else for a few days. A couple of hundred dollars should more than cover it." He looked at Grant. "Does that sound better?"

Scottlyn met his gaze. "Grant?"

Grant looked down into Scottlyn's blue eyes. The hope and excitement shining there should have filled him with happiness. Instead, he worried about the crash waiting around the curve if their doubts proved true. *This whole situation makes the skin between my shoulders itch.* Scottlyn's eyes pleaded with him. He nodded a yes with a resigned sigh. *What choice do I have?*

A relieved breath swooshed from Scottlyn's lungs. "Thank you." She pulled out of his arms. "I'm going to go tell her about the house. I know she'll be thrilled."

Grant watched as she nearly danced out of the room. He glanced over when Harold Cole came to stand by his side. "Thanks."

"For?"

"For taking some of the heat off of me. There was no way I was going to say yes to a thousand dollars."

"I didn't think so. I'm glad I could offer you an alternative. Frankly, I'd have given her the two hundred dollars if it kept that woman in town for a few days."

Grant raised his eyebrows. "Whatever for?"

"Have you heard the old saying about keeping your friends close and your enemies closer?"

Grant nodded.

"There's something very wrong about this, and I want Jocelyn Rich where I can keep an eye on her until we can sort it out."

CHAPTER SIX

Jocelyn woke up Saturday morning, flat on her stomach in a strange bed, and surrounded by pillows. She raised herself up on an elbow and scooped long blonde hair out of her face.

"Where...?"

Details of the previous day flooded into her sleep-fogged brain. *William's house.* She flopped onto her back. *My house.*

"My house." She said the words aloud, trying them on for size. Her unbridled laughter split the early morning solitude. "My house! Oh wait till Andrew hears this." She grabbed the phone from the bedside table and punched in the number.

"Morning, doll. How did it go?"

"It's my house!"

"What?"

"William's house, Andrew. This big old rambling house sitting in the middle of three acres is mine."

A second or two of silence greeted her news. "Are you high?"

"Only on life and good news."

"Want to share?"

She shoved pillows against the headboard and settled back. "William never filed for divorce."

"What?"

"Surprised me too. And it gets better. He never changed the will he made right after Scottlyn was born. The house, and everything in it, is mine, along with half of whatever money he left behind.

"Yeah?"

"I just scored us the biggest payday of our lives and all you can say is yeah? This has to be the biggest game changer in the history of scams." Jocelyn paused for a second to offer a prayer of gratitude on the altar of avarice. The thought of living off whatever cash she could con out of Scottlyn evaporated. "The rules have changed...big time. I think I need to stick here for a while and play the doting mother and grandmother until the legal stuff pans out."

Andrew groaned into the phone. "That could take months. Have you forgotten that we need some immediate cash? And may I remind you, you don't do kids."

The reminder soured her mood. She drummed her fingers on the mattress. *Why did he have to be so impatient and shortsighted?* "I can handle the kid in small doses for the sort of payday this could net us. As for our cash flow problems, let me see if I can find some things around here that won't be missed. I'll call you in a day or two."

"I guess that works. I'll be missing you by then."

Jocelyn grinned at the lust she heard in his voice. "You just keep my side of the bed warm for me."

She said good-bye, stretched, and rolled out of the bed. Food and exploration beckoned. She pulled on the pair of jeans and a baggy T-shirt Scottlyn had brought over the night before. Borrowed from Diana, whoever that was. The fit wasn't the best, but it beat the dress and heels she'd worn all day yesterday. She slipped her feet into a pair of flip-flops with a sigh of relief. The new heels might be her current pride and joy, but they'd pinched her toes unmercifully by the end of the long day yesterday.

She slid them under the edge of the bed. She hadn't splurged on something so nice in a long time, and she needed to take care of them. *I can have whatever I want soon.* The thought made her giddy.

Jocelyn fussed in front of the mirror. Always conscious of the role she played, today she went less for the grieving widow and more for the adoring grandmother. She considered leaving her face bare of makeup, but in the end, vanity won out. She might have to play a grandma, but she refused to look like one.

A search of the cabinets in the kitchen produced some coffee. Once it was brewing, she assessed possible breakfast choices, deciding on toast slathered in butter and strawberry preserves.

Jocelyn took both to the table, sipped, chewed, and tried to figure out the next step in her altered plan of action.

The way she saw it, manipulating Scottlyn would be a breeze, even long term. That boyfriend of hers would be a different story though. With every one of his looks, he probed for a flaw in her story. She had three options. Find a way to get into his good graces, find a way to shut him up, or find a way to drive a wedge between him and Scottlyn. She balled up her napkin and tossed it in the direction of the waste can. "I'm not real picky about which one works."

~ * ~

"Fiddle!" Scottlyn grabbed a napkin and sopped up the sloshed coffee.

"Nervous?" Diana asked.

"What was the first clue?" Scottlyn stared at the dark stain spreading across her light pink shirt. She pulled the wet fabric away from her skin, scooted back from the table, and stripped the soiled shirt off as she walked into the laundry room that adjoined the kitchen. She spread the shirt out on top of the closed washer and sprayed it with a stain remover, marveling at the way her hands shook in the process.

Diana's voice drifted in from the other room. "I finished your laundry while you were at your father's house yesterday. There's a stack of clean shirts on the dryer."

Scottlyn grabbed a replacement. *What would I do without Diana?* The thought gave her pause. *I have two mothers now.* She smoothed the shirt and went back to the kitchen. She stopped behind Diana's chair and wrapped the woman in a hug. "Have I told you lately how very much I love you?"

Diana patted her hand. "It was just a load of laundry, sweetheart. They were already dry. All I did was fold them."

"Today." Scottlyn let her go and circled back to her chair. "It's so much more than that. It's the little things you do for me and Mercie every day. We have a roof over our heads because of you, and not once have you made us feel like you regretted the decision to make a home for us. No one has ever loved me like that. I'm so blessed to have you in my life."

The older woman's eyes misted. "That's a very mutual feeling, sweetheart. You aren't the only one blessed by our cobbled-together family." Diana took her empty coffee cup to the sink, rinsed it, and put it in the dishwasher. When she turned around, she leaned against the cabinet. "Tell me about your mother."

Scottlyn ran her fingers around the edge of her mug, her eyes focused on the creamy chocolate flavored brew she favored. "She's...sad." Scottlyn took a drink of the lukewarm beverage. "And lost, and alone." She lifted her gaze. "Those are dismal words, aren't they? I need to find a way to change them to happier adjectives."

Diana crossed her arms. "Do you think that's your responsibility?"

Scottlyn studied Diana's expression. There was something guarded in the older woman's face. She looked a lot like Grant had looked last night. Just a little pained by the whole situation. Why couldn't they just be happy for her? Scottlyn's shoulder lifted. "Maybe not my responsibility, but she's my mother." She tilted her head. "I don't want you to be threatened by that. Having her here won't change our relationship. I need to get to know her...help where I can. Doesn't the Bible say to honor my parents?"

The corners of Diana's mouth lifted in a quick smile. "Yes, it does. But it also says to be wise as a serpent and as harmless as a dove." She crossed the room, reclaimed her seat, and took Scottlyn's hand in hers. "I'm not worried about our relationship, sweetheart. I just want you to be careful."

Scottlyn's brows drew together into a frown. "What do you mean?"

"I wish I knew. I just feel the need to tell you to be careful. Be watchful. Be cautious. Keep your ears tuned to the small voice inside your heart. Satan doesn't always come at us as a roaring lion. Sometimes he shows up meek and mild...sad, lost, and alone, wearing the face of the one thing we've always wanted."

Scottlyn squeezed Diana's hand. "I'll be careful, but right now, I have to pick up Mercie and take Mom shopping. She can't spend two or three days in a single pair of jeans."

An hour later, Scottlyn parked her red Rav4 in the driveway of her father's home. She looked into the backseat where Mercie sat, strapped into her car seat. "Remember what I said?"

Mercie's blue eyes crinkled in a smile. "That I have to be on my bery best 'havior." She frowned at the strange house. "Because I'm meeting Grandma Joyce."

Scottlyn smiled. "That's close enough." She got out and unbuckled her daughter. They went up the walk together, and Scottlyn opened the door a crack. "Mom?"

"Come on in, baby."

The door swung open, and Scottlyn led Mercie inside. She gave her mother a quick hug. "Did you get some rest last night?"

"Yes, thanks. The bed is great." Jocelyn stopped and looked down. "And who is this little cutie?"

"This is Mercie, your granddaughter."

When Jocelyn stooped down, Mercie held out her right hand. Both of the women laughed.

Scottlyn put a hand on Mercie's shoulder." I told her to be on her best behavior."

Jocelyn shook the small hand and patted the child on the head. She stood up and faced Scottlyn. "I just fixed a second cup of coffee. Would you like a cup before we head out?"

Mercie tugged at her hand before she could answer. She pointed at the TV across the room. "Can I watch cartoons?"

Scottlyn looked from her daughter to her mother. Neither one seemed very interested in getting to know the other. She pushed the disappointment aside. A three-year-old and a woman just out of prison...a little awkwardness with each other seemed normal. Hopefully some of that would melt as they spent the day together. She smiled at her mother. "Coffee sounds great. Just let me get Mercie settled, and I'll join you in the kitchen."

She found a station running *Dora the Explorer*. "Is this good?"

Mercie crawled up onto the sofa and clapped her hands. "Yes!"

"OK. Sit here until we're ready to go." She went into the kitchen and found her mother sitting at the table, her head bent over the comic section of the morning paper.

Jocelyn waved at the coffee pot. "Help yourself. I'm just catching up on my daily reading."

Scottlyn grinned. She liked the comics best, too. As a rule, the news was too depressing. "What's your favorite?"

"Garfield." Her mother answered without hesitation. "Love that sassy cat. Yours?"

Scottlyn looked over her mother's shoulder. "I'm with you. The cat is hilarious. I miss Snoopy though."

"Mommy, look."

Scottlyn turned around and saw Mercie standing in the doorway. Her shoes had been abandoned, and she teetered forward in a pair of spiky black heels. "What have you got?"

Jocelyn turned as well. "My shoes!"

Mercie looked up at the shouted words, tripped, and fell. The shoes came off of the child's small feet. One landed with a broken heel.

Jocelyn jumped from the table. "Look what you've done!" She grabbed her shoes and glared down at Mercie.

Scottlyn swooped in to grab her baby just before Jocelyn's raised hand descended.

CHAPTER SEVEN

"What do you think you're doing?"

Jocelyn lowered her hand. *Not good.* "I'm sorry, I wouldn't have smacked her. It's the..."—*think fast girlfriend*—"...the prison thing." *Yeah, that's good.* "We had so little there to call our own, and I just bought those...and...I'm sorry." She looked at the sniveling brat who'd just trashed a pair of one hundred dollar shoes. *What should I do?*

She patted the child's head. "It's OK"—she dredged up a word—"honey, don't cry." Jocelyn swallowed. "Grandma's sorry."

Scottlyn nudged her aside and carried the squalling kid into the living room.

Jocelyn stood in the hallway holding the ruined shoes. *If you don't do something quick, your plan is going to look like your shoes.* She edged forward and peeked into the next room. Scottlyn sat on the sofa rocking her daughter while the little girl sniffed, smearing snot and tears into the front of her mother's shirt. Jocelyn shuddered.

"I'm sorry, Mama. They were pretty."

"Yes, but they weren't yours, and you didn't have permission. What have we said about that?"

"That I need to ask before I touch."

"That's right, and now you need to apologize."

An apology? Jocelyn ducked back around the corner,

crossed her arms, and leaned against the wall. Where was the thrashing? *My mother would have yanked me up by the scruff of my neck and whaled the tar out of me.* Kids had no respect these days. She struggled for composure. If the kid was going to apologize, she'd have to accept it. If she was going to regain her footing with Scottlyn, she'd have to do a whole lot more than that. She looked at the shoes as an idea formed. *Oh, who cares, they're ruined anyway.* She straightened, gripped the shoes tighter, and stepped into the room.

Mercie scrambled off Scottlyn's lap and raced to meet her halfway. She stopped with her hands behind her back and her head bowed. "Your shoes are bery pretty. I'm sorry I broke them."

"It's OK. We all make mistakes." She knelt in front of the child. "You think they're pretty?"

The kid nodded.

Jocelyn pulled in a deep breath. *I can't believe I'm doing this.* She gave the heel of the unbroken shoe a quick, hard twist. The heel snapped off, leaving her with a pair of expensive, useless flats. She handed them to Mercie. "Here you go. Now you can wear them without tripping."

Scottlyn's gasp filled the room. "I was going to take them and have the broken one repaired."

Now she says... Jocelyn let her hair fall forward to hide the frustration on her face. She forced words through clenched teeth. "No big deal." When she looked up, she had a smile pasted in place. "It's just a silly pair of shoes." She pushed herself to her feet while the kid paraded around the room, wearing her new prize.

Jocelyn joined Scottlyn on the sofa. "I owe you an apology. I overreacted."

"I can accept that. Mercie was in the wrong, but so was I. I know better than to leave a curious three-year-old unsupervised in a new place." Scottlyn drew herself up and looked Jocelyn in the eye. "We need to understand each other. Mercie is my responsibility, and I'm doing the best I can with her. I've never laid a hand on her in anger, and I won't stand by and allow anyone else to do so."

Jocelyn nodded. *She-bear and her cub.* "I have a lot to learn about being a mother and a grandmother. I'm hoping you'll give me some time."

The smile she received in return trembled a bit. "That's what today is all about, right? Getting to know each other?"

"Absolutely."

"Then let's get started." Scottlyn turned to her daughter. "Mercie, it's time to go. You need to put your tennis shoes back on."

Mercie came running. "Shopping at the big stores?"

"Yes, ma'am."

The youngster jumped up and down. "The toy place too?"

Scottlyn caught the child's chin in her hand. "I'm afraid not. You lost that privilege when you didn't mind Mommy. We have to replace grandma's shoes, and I don't have the money for both."

"But..." The little girl's chin quivered, and her blue eyes filled with tears.

Jocelyn almost felt sorry for her.

"Don't whine." Scottlyn's voice was firm.

"Yes, ma'am." Mercie's shoulders slumped as she pulled free of her mother's hand and went to fetch her shoes.

"That's not necessary."

"Yes it is." Scottlyn told her. "Mercie needs to learn that her actions come with consequences. Sacrificing the toy she wanted today will help her remember that just because something is pretty doesn't mean it's hers to play with."

Jocelyn started to object a second time but swallowed it back. What did she know about being a mother? She watched from beneath her lashes as Scottlyn tied the kid's shoes and left the room to take her to the bathroom. Mercie might be learning about actions and consequences, but Jocelyn was learning as well. She'd found a backbone underneath Scottlyn's tender exterior. She wasn't entirely sure that was a good thing.

~ * ~

The ticking of the living room clock sounded thunderous in the silence that followed Scottlyn's announcement Saturday night.

"You did what?"

She crossed her arms and paced the length of Diana's living room, putting some space between her and her angry fiancé. "Why is this a big deal?"

Grant looked at her like she'd grown a second head. "Why is this a...?" He ran his hand through his hair. "Who are you and where is my level-headed girlfriend?"

Scottlyn narrowed her eyes at him.

He shook his head. "I can't believe we're even having this conversation."

"Neither can I," she said. "It's a hundred and fifty dollars, not a thousand."

"It's three hundred fifty, and we agreed on two hundred."

"Oh, we agreed all right." She put her hands on her hips and leaned forward. "After I practically had to pry the debit card out of your hands."

This time it was Grant's eyes that narrowed to slits.

"That's not fair."

"And neither was the fact that Mercie trashed her shoes." Scottlyn did her best to calm her tone of voice. She held out her hands. "Grant, you should have seen the look on her face. It was so sad, like something inside her broke right along with the shoes. I don't know why they meant so much to her, but I had to replace them."

"I understand that you felt you had an obligation. What I don't understand is how you think it's OK to spend the additional money without talking to me first."

Scottlyn raised her eyebrows and tilted her head. "That's how it's going to be after we're married? I have to ask for permission to buy a pair of shoes?"

Grant's eyes closed, and he clasped both hands around the back of his neck. "You know better than that," he mumbled. He opened his eyes and pinned her with a stare. "It's a joint account set aside for a specific reason. We promised to discuss any withdrawals before they were made. We discussed two-hundred dollars. I agreed because I know this is important to you. You withdrew three-hundred-fifty. I'm not asking you to account for every dollar you spend, but I am asking for the same consideration I'd give you if the situation was reversed."

His reminders let the air out of her arguments. She accepted the truth. "You're right." Scottlyn moved toward him. She slipped her arms around his waist, and his eyes bored into hers as she looked up. "I messed up, and I'm sorry." Her forehead came to rest on his chest.

"I'm just..." Scottlyn sighed. "Part of me is afraid that she'll take off again, and I'm trying to do everything I can think of not to give her an excuse."

Grant's snort echoed in her ears as his arms tightened around her. "I don't think that's a problem."

Scottlyn leaned back and met his eyes again. "What do

you mean?" She frowned when his expression tightened.

"Scottie, can we be honest with each other?"

She nodded.

He took a deep breath. "Don't you think her return to Sabor is just a little too convenient?"

"No." A short answer as she tried to pull out of his arms.

His embrace tightened. "Hear me out, OK?"

Scottlyn stopped struggling. "I'll listen, but will you let me go?"

Grant eased his arms apart, tipped her chin up, and brushed her lips with a kiss. "I love you."

"I love you, too." She took a step back and clasped her hand behind her back. "Say what you need to say."

"Baby, my heart breaks for you right now. You lost your Dad right when you were hoping to reconcile with him. I've never been without my parents, so I can't say I understand how it feels to lose one, but I'm trying to be sensitive and supportive...trying hard to understand the feelings you described yesterday afternoon. Then this woman shows up out of the blue, claiming to be your long lost mother."

Scottlyn raised her chin. "She *is* my mother."

Grant held up his hands. "OK. But can you take a step away from emotional and look at it objectively? She comes back to town with a sob story no one can prove on the very day you buried your father to lay claim to half an inheritance that should all go to you and Mercie." He shook his head. "That's pretty hard to swallow."

He could tell by the flush in her face that he'd said the wrong thing. Scottlyn crossed her arms. "What is it with you and money tonight?"

"This isn't about..."

"Oh, knock it off." She stalked across the room before

turning to look at him again. "When did everything become about money? First you get torqued because I spent a little more than we agreed on, and now you're worried about an inheritance neither of us even knew existed four days ago. I've never known you to be greedy."

"Greedy?" He frowned at her. "Beyond our joint account agreement, I could care less. The only thing I'm worried about is you and Mercie. You're so...blinded by this *miracle*, and ready to believe anything this woman has to say, I'm afraid you're going to get hurt. If I can prevent that, I will. It has nothing to do with money."

He walked across the room and took her hands. "You're going to be spending a lot of time with her. I'm just asking you to keep your eyes open."

Scottlyn jerked her hands free. "And now you're jealous."

Grant frowned. "What are you talking about?"

"You're worried about me spending too much money on, and too much time with, a mother I haven't seen in seventeen years. That's more than a little petty."

"I never said that."

"You didn't have to."

They stared at each other over crossed arms.

Grant ran his hands down his face. "I'm going home."

"Good. I'm going to call my mother."

Grant shook his head and left without another word.

Scottlyn retreated to her room and slammed her door. The noise woke Mercie. Scottlyn fumed on the inside while she worked to get the three-year-old back to sleep. *Just who does he think he is?*

CHAPTER EIGHT

Scottlyn crawled out of bed on Sunday morning, exhausted from a restless night and heavy-hearted over her fight with Grant. She dressed for church on autopilot, the questions of the previous night still ringing in her heart. The coffee she hoped would jump start her day never even made it to her lips before Mercie scrambled into her booster seat at the kitchen table.

She gave her mom a dazzling smile. "Mommy, my tummy is bery, bery hungry. Can I have my cereal now?"

"Good morning, baby." Scottlyn put the cup aside and opened the pantry. She reached for the box of the chocolate flavored rice cereal the three-year-old loved so much. It was Mercie's Sunday morning treat and only allowed once a week. The weight of the box told Scottlyn that it was almost empty. *Great.* With everything going on this week, she'd forgotten to go to the store.

Mercie bounced in her seat. "Mommy."

"Just a minute." Scottlyn shuffled through boxes and found a box of plain rice cereal. *Humm...maybe she'll be intrigued.* She removed both boxes, poured up a bowl of the plain, mixed in the remains of the cocoa, and set it in front of her daughter.

The three-year-old's sunny disposition melted like ice cream on a hot day. She looked at Scottlyn.

Scottlyn offered her a weak smile. "It's polka dot

crispies."

"My tummy needs Choco Crispies."

Scottlyn drew in a calming breath. She pointed to the stingy brown specks floating in the milk. "There they are."

Mercie's bottom lip came out in a pout. "Yuck!" She pushed the bowl away. Milk slopped over the edge, puddled on the table, and dripped onto the floor." She jutted out her bottom lip and stared at her mother. "Choco Crispies."

Scottlyn put her hands on her hips and looked at the mess. "Mercie Delynn Rich. That is more than enough. You will eat what I—"

"Good morning, ladies." Diana breezed into the kitchen. She put an arm around Scottlyn and peered into Mercie's bowl. "My goodness. Where did you get leopard flavored cereal?"

Mercie crossed her arms, but her frown eased a bit as she studied the contents of the bowl. "Leopard?"

"Oh, yes. I think that's what people eat when they go on safari to hunt leopards. Do you know what a leopard is?"

Mercie shook her head.

Diana picked up the spoon and held it out to the three-year-old. "You clean your bowl, and we'll go look them up on my computer when you're done. While you do that, Mommy and I are going to go have a visit in the living room."

"OK!" Mercie grabbed the spoon and attacked her breakfast with fresh gusto.

Diana hooked an arm through Scottlyn's and led her into the next room. She motioned to the sofa and took a seat once Scottlyn sat. "What's up with you?"

Scottlyn rubbed at her temples and the headache that

pounded there. "She sloshed milk all over the floor."

"Honey, she's three. Mess-making is what three-year-olds do best." Diana raised a hand to stem Scottlyn's objections. "And I get it that she was acting out in the process...that's the second best thing that three-year-olds do. But it's the first time I've ever seen you that close to losing your temper with her. What gives?"

Scottlyn leaned her head back against the sofa cushions, weary to the bone. "Grant and I had a huge fight last night. I said some horrible things, and he left mad." She crossed her arms over her eyes. "I didn't get any sleep." Her voice cracked. "And then we were out of Choco Crispies."

"The straw that broke the camel's back."

"Something like that."

"You want to talk about the fight?"

Scottlyn sat up and swiped at her eyes. "He hates my mom."

"Oh, sweetheart, no he doesn't."

"Diana, he does." She shoved herself up and paced in front of the sofa. "You haven't seen them together. He's gruff when he speaks to her. He questions everything she says or does. Now, he's questioning everything I do for her." She turned to face the only mother she'd ever known until two days ago. "I thought he loved me, but if he can't accept my mother..." She finger combed her hair from her face. "What am I supposed to do? I love them both."

"If you can stand there and honestly say you have doubts about how Grant feels about you, you need more than a good night's sleep." Diana took a deep breath. "Do you want my honest opinion?"

Scottlyn nodded.

"You've had a week that would knock anyone back a

few steps. Grief, excitement, and everything in between. If you weren't feeling a little off center, I'd be worried about you more than I already am. You never had the chance to know your mother, and all at once, here she is. You're excited about a future that includes her. You have every right to those feelings, but...love? I don't think so."

"Diana..."

"Hear me out and be honest with yourself. Do you love Jocelyn Rich, or do you love what Jocelyn Rich represents? The person, or the idea of having a mother? When you can sort that out for yourself, you'll get a better feel for where Grant...and I...stand in all of this."

Scottlyn sat down. "What do you mean?"

"Grant and I both love you. We both want to protect you. Because of that, we'll both be a bit more cautious than you. And that's a good thing. You need people looking out for you when you're too close to a situation to see it clearly."

"What's to see? She's my mother."

Diana tilted her head, and Scottlyn saw a hint of frost in her blue eyes. "And Gabe and Penny are Mercie's grandparents. A couple of years ago, when they suddenly decided that they were ready to be a part of Mercie's life, she would have accepted them without hesitation. But you didn't allow that right off. Why?"

Scottlyn raised her hands and dropped them to her sides. "Because I didn't know them, because they had done some despicable things, because they were in a position to hurt her like no one else could. They had to prove to me...that they were worthy of her...love."

Diana raised her eyebrows. "And there you have it."

~ * ~

238

Sabor's Faith Tabernacle was packed with worshipers. The sanctuary echoed with enthusiastic praise and worship music. Scottlyn's gaze swept the crowd, looking for Grant. She frowned when she didn't see him. *Fine, let him sit home and pout. I have better things to do.*

Scottlyn lifted her hands and her face to heaven. *Father, thank You. I've been so caught up in Daddy and the funeral, so heartbroken about losing him, that I haven't taken the time to thank You for the one good thing that came out of that. Thank you for giving my mother back to me.* Her prayer barely made it out of her heart before the sense of foreboding that she'd experienced off and on all week returned to tie her stomach in knots. She rubbed at the spot where the agitation lodged. *What's up with this nagging sense of...?*

Before she could finish her thought, Pastor Robbins took his place behind the pulpit. He looked out over the crowd as the last notes of the worship music faded. "My, it's good to have everyone here this morning. If you're visiting with us today, I hope you'll find something here that makes you feel at home." He made a motion. "You can be seated." While the congregation took their seats, the old pastor took off his glasses and polished them with a handkerchief. He settled them back into place and leaned across the pulpit on his forearms.

"How many of you have ever worked hard on a project for your boss, only to have him decide he wanted something different at the last moment?" He nodded as hands went up all over the building. "Good, then you'll know how I'm feeling today. I studied all week and had my sermon ready for today, and sometime in the night, God changed my mind." His eyes roamed from one side of the building to the other. "At times like this, I just have to trust His leading and believe that someone here this morning needs to hear what God laid on my heart."

He opened his Bible. "Today we're going to spend some time in Proverbs." He looked up and smiled. "You know, the Bible says that Solomon was the wisest man that ever lived. Far be it from me to disagree with the Good Book, but I'm not sure that title belongs to any man who gets involved with more than nine hundred women...at the same time." He paused until the laughter died down.

"We live in a world where honest people seem to be in the minority. Where people would rather cheat you out of a dollar than earn it honestly." He stopped and held up his cell phone. "I get at least four calls a week from people claiming to be from my credit card company, offering to lower my interest rate. All they need is some personal information to get started." He shook his head. "Problem is that I've spoken to all the companies that I have accounts with, and they've assured me that they will never call me with offers like this. As a result, I've started blocking the numbers, but they just keep coming up with new ones." He slipped the phone back into his pocket.

"Deception isn't a new concept. In Ecclesiastes, Solomon assures us that there is nothing new under the sun. And he's right. We can trace fraud all the way back to the Old Testament. Jacob worked for seven years for his wife and woke up to find they'd slipped the older sister into his bed." He chuckled. "I've always wondered about that. I know they didn't have electricity in those tents, but they had candlelight.

"What I'm trying to do is make a case for wisdom in our daily lives. The second verse of the first chapter in Proverbs cautions us to 'know wisdom and instruction: to perceive the words of understanding.' We need to get better acquainted with the wisdom God promised to give to all who ask."

Scottlyn squirmed in her seat as the old preacher's words hit home and intensified the discomfort in her heart. She lost the rest of the sermon under the weight of uncertainty. *Father, what am I missing? I know it has to do with Mom, but...* She replayed the last two days in her memory. Yes, there had been a few moments of confusion, but they didn't know each other. Wasn't that to be expected?

Her heart cracked with the knowledge that she might have been more hasty than wise. Not that she didn't believe Jocelyn was her mother. Harold Cole had verified that, and the resemblance was too much to deny. But maybe Scottlyn could entertain the idea that Jocelyn's return was as conveniently timed as Grant claimed. Maybe things weren't as cut-and-dried as they appeared at first glance.

A tear streaked down her face, and she swiped it away.

From her place in the pew beside her, Diana laid a hand on her arm. "Scottlyn?"

Scottlyn shook her head and squeezed Diana's hand. "I'm OK." And she was. She planned to spend the rest of the day with her mother. She'd take the pastor's advice and be quietly attentive to everything her mother said, every expression on her face. Scottlyn would do this, because everything inside of her wanted to be able to cling to this relationship. Now that the questions had been raised, trying and failing to prove that her mother was a liar seemed like the only way to get that done.

CHAPTER NINE

Scottlyn nosed her vehicle into a parking space in front of the bank, turned off the ignition, and hit the redial button on her phone. When the call went to Grant's voice mail for the twentieth time, she swiped the connection closed without leaving a message. *No point. I've left at least ten over the last day and a half.* She sat for a few seconds and stared into space. Grant was angry with her, she got that, but ignoring her calls wasn't the way to settle their argument. She needed to apologize, needed to tell him that she was being more careful about...well, she still didn't know what she was supposed to be looking for, but she was looking.

So far that quest hadn't produced a single thing to make her suspicious. Scottlyn didn't know whether to be pleased or more confused. She'd spent most of the previous day with her mother. They'd looked through old picture albums while Scottlyn shared memories from her childhood. When the subject moved to the rape that left her pregnant with Mercie and her father's actions in the aftermath, her mother had been visibly sympathetic, and in contrast, happy about Scottlyn's upcoming marriage to Grant.

And though her mother had plenty of questions about Grant, it had all seemed the proper response for a woman getting newly acquainted with her daughter. The single moment of sadness in the whole day came only when

Mom realized all of the pictures of her had gone missing from the albums. Dad must have destroyed them. *He was such a contradiction in extremes. Never divorcing the woman who'd walked out of his life, but removing every reminder of her existence.*

Scottlyn returned to the present and fingered the new key on her key ring. Harold called earlier and asked her to pick up a copy of the paperwork giving her access to her father's safe deposit box. She watched the entrance of the bank, people coming and going, each one with their own story, their own mission. *I wonder if anyone would trade their task for mine.* She'd be willing to tackle just about anything in exchange for emptying Dad's safe deposit box. She drew in a fortifying breath and pushed out of the car. Stalling wouldn't get it done.

Three bank employees and two security checks later, Scottlyn sat at a tiny table in a little room. The metal box rested in front of her. Her hands remained clasped in her lap, the only sound in the room her forlorn whisper. "Oh, Daddy, I feel like I'm violating your privacy. I'm not worried about what's in here, but opening it just makes your absence feel a little more permanent." She giggled even as a tear slid down her face. *Death is pretty permanent.* She clapped a hand over her mouth and looked around. *Get a grip. People will think you're a loon!*

Scottlyn lifted the lid. Unlike the dramatic moments portrayed in the movies, she did not find a stack of one hundred dollar bills, a falsified passport, and a handgun. She lifted the contents out piece by piece and lined them up on the table.

The first was a gold pocket watch. It had a chain attached to a small loop at the top and a raised image of an eagle on the back. The case was worn smooth by the many hands that had handled it over the years. She found the latch, opened the front, and squinted at the engraving.

Warren Rich 1883. Hmm... "Daddy was William. Grandpa Rich died before I was born, but his name was Albert." Scottlyn did the math in her head. "One hundred thirty-three years. Warren could have been my great-grandfather." Scottlyn laid it aside. *Grant and I might have a son to pass it down to someday. If he's still speaking to me.*

Next, she unwound a rubber band holding a brown manila folder closed. Inside she found a bundle of legal documents pertaining to her father's estate. Relief that her future was just a little more secure warred with regret over the things left unspoken between father and daughter. She swallowed past her constricted throat, refolded the documents, and pulled out the remaining items. Her parent's marriage license and a stack of birth certificates. One for her father, her grandmother, and her grandfather. She grinned when she examined the one belonging to Albert. Warren was indeed listed as her great-grandfather.

Scottlyn refolded everything and secured it back into the folder. She'd take these to Harold. The last item from the box was a thick white envelope. Scottlyn lifted the flap and shook the contents onto the table. Pictures scattered across the smooth top. She bit down on a smile even as laughter bubbled in her throat. "The missing pictures. He didn't throw them away."

She gathered them into a stack. It was snapshots of her parent's early life together. Pictures of her mother as a bride. Shots taken on a beach maybe from Mom and Dad's honeymoon. Images of a much younger Jocelyn holding a newborn. Scottlyn's finger shook as she traced the figures.

"Mom, look at you, so young and beautiful, and you look so happy." She turned the picture into the light, looking for evidence of the stress Jocelyn had cited.

Maybe there were a few tension lines around her eyes, but the photos were nearly twenty years old, it was hard to tell. She flipped to the last picture in the stack. *That's odd, it's...* She scraped the edge with a nail and the picture separated into three. Her breath whooshed out of her lungs. Her pulse accelerated, and a fine film of sweat coated her forehead and the back of her neck.

The images that looked back at her from the photo hidden in the middle were almost identical to what she saw in her mirror every day. That wasn't what took her breath. Two teenaged girls posed in the picture on a summer day. They had ice cream cones in their hands... and matching eyes and smiles. She flipped the picture over, barely able to read the faded writing due to the trembling in her fingers.

Jocelynn and Marilyn, 1984, age 15.

The picture fluttered to the table. Her mother had a twin sister.

~ * ~

Grant removed his glasses and wiped sweat from his face with a napkin he'd saved from his breakfast. Cozumel and Oklahoma might share a time zone, but the late spring temperatures of home didn't hold a candle to the humid, tropical heat he found himself in.

I can't believe I'm actually doing this. Harold Cole had a friend who knew somebody, who had a brother who knew somebody with a private jet and overnight business in Cozumel. They'd allowed him to tag along, landing late last night. They were scheduled to fly out right after lunch. Grant had about four hours to find the information he needed.

An ocean breeze ruffled his hair and pulled his eyes

back to the turquoise water the Caribbean was so famous for. In the distance he could see at least three of the mammoth cruise ships that brought a steady flow of tourist to this little piece of heaven. Grant smiled. Scottlyn didn't know it yet, but there were two tickets in his dresser drawer at home. One of them had her name on it. He couldn't wait to use them in...he opened a countdown app on his phone...fifty-eight days.

The phone buzzed with an incoming call, and Scottlyn's number lit the screen. He let it go to voice mail. She'd been calling him since yesterday afternoon. Ignoring her calls wouldn't win him any points, but neither would knowing he'd come to Cozumel without her. The reasons behind the trip would only add to her irritation.

He shrugged off the worry over her reaction as he made his way to the taxi stand in front of the hotel. She needed to accept the fact that it was his job to protect her. If she couldn't come to terms with that...well, they'd argue about it when he got home without the long distance charges.

Jocelyn Rich. Everything about that woman rubbed him the wrong way. He couldn't explain it, and he couldn't live with it. Despite Scottlyn's accusations, his reaction had nothing to do with money or jealously. He had parents. They made occasional demands on his time. He loved them. Why would he begrudge Scottlyn the same?

And money? Grant shook his head. He had a brand new degree in journalism. He made a decent living as the rookie reporter for one of the local television stations. *Rookie reporter* wasn't his dream, but it was a step on the ladder to the job that was his dream...investigative reporter.

In addition to protecting the woman he loved, Grant

viewed this as an opportunity to try out the techniques he'd learned in school. There was a story here, and he intended to find it.

He took his place at the back of the line and waited his turn for a cab.

"Where would you like to go this morning, amigo?" The man wore white shorts and a button up shirt. He waved his hand to motion for the next cab in line, and even at eight-thirty in the morning, Grant noticed a patch of sweat shadowing the area between the man's shoulder blades.

"Where would I go to research old court records?"

The man raised his dark eyebrows, obviously caught off guard by the unusual request.

Grant hurried to reassure him. "I'm a journalist doing some leg work on a story. I'd be grateful if you could point me in the right direction."

The attendant smiled. "Si, Senior." He opened the back door of the taxi and spoke to the driver in rapid-fire Spanish while Grant climbed inside.

The driver nodded, reset his trip meter, and headed down the looping drive that led from the hotel to the main road.

Grant settled back in the seat and took in the scenery of downtown Cozumel, shops on one side, the ocean on the other. He'd considered making the embassy his first stop, but privacy laws would keep anyone official from answering his unofficial questions. He didn't have the time or money to waste trying to find someone willing to talk to him.

He didn't know anything about Mexican privacy laws but hoped they weren't as strict as American ones. He was betting on the language barrier working in his favor. The words *American journalist* might open a door or two, along with the flash of a few American dollars. He closed his eyes and hedged that bet with a quick prayer. *Father, I need You to give me favor and guide my search. Truth comes from You, and there's a truth to this situation that I need to find. You know my heart. My only interest is protecting Scottlyn. Please help me do that.*

The cab jerked to a stop in front of a line of old buildings. The driver pointed while rattling off a stream of words that Grant's high school Spanish didn't cover. *I hope someone in there speaks a little English.* He paid the driver, crossed his fingers, and entered the building.

The process was surprisingly simple. He gave the clerk Jocelyn's name and the approximate dates of her trial and imprisonment. An hour later he was seated at a table with a large cardboard box. His excitement built as he removed the lid. Anticipation collided with reality when everything he removed from the box was written in Spanish. *Well, duh!*

At the bottom of the box was a bag of personal items. He opened a small purse to find a set of keys, a crumpled plane ticket in Jocelyn's name, a dried up lipstick, and a billfold. An examination of the billfold produced a driver's license that expired in 1999 and a couple of faded pictures. Both were shots of a young woman who looked amazingly like Scottlyn. The woman was holding a newborn.

Grant replaced everything in the bag. *Shouldn't these have been returned to Jocelyn on her release last month?* Grant rubbed the back of his neck. Sending Jocelyn home and keeping this stuff here made no sense. He started the chore of stacking everything back into the box, looking for anything to help explain the mystery.

He tapped a stack of papers together, and an envelope slipped free. One word was written on the front. *Scottlyn.*

His curiosity was almost unbearable. He held it in his hand and weighed the possibilities. Whatever lay hidden in there likely held the answers to many of his questions, but it was addressed to Scottlyn, not him. In the end he laid it aside, unwilling to break Scottlyn's trust.

A final piece of paper caught his eye. It read *El Certificado de la Muerta.* His Spanish might be rusty, but the words were pretty clear nonetheless. It was a death certificate.

His hands shook as he struggled to make out the details. The name on the certificate and the dates jumped out at him. Jocelyn Rich. August 1998.

His heart hammered in his chest. Vindication and sorrow warred as the piece of paper slipped to the table. "Oh, babe!"

CHAPTER TEN

Scottlyn sat in the darkened sanctuary of Faith Tabernacle with her head bowed. Prayer usually came easy, especially here. Not so much this morning. She looked up with tears in her eyes. "I don't know what to ask You for. I'm more than a little afraid of the answer." Her whispered words hung in the hushed atmosphere of the building.

"I was so sure You brought Mom back into my life as a comfort when You took Daddy away. I didn't think I needed to pray about it...other than to thank You." Scottlyn wiped her face. "Dear God, is this person really my Mom?" Her shoulders lifted in a forlorn shrug. "Who prays that sort of prayer?" A sob worked its way up from someplace deep in her heart. "I guess, me."

Scottlyn crossed her arms on the back of the pew in front of her and rested her head on them. She lost track of time as she wept out her worries and fears.

"Scottlyn?"

She jerked upright, grabbed a crumpled tissue from her lap, and mopped her face. "Pastor."

"I thought I recognized your car." He stepped around the side of the pew and took a seat next to her. "I'm sorry if I interrupted you, but you sounded so unhappy. Is this about your father?"

Scottlyn shook her head. "Not really...at least not directly."

"You and Grant fighting?"

"Yeah, but that's not it either." She opened her bag and held out a picture.

Pastor Robbins studied it. "Do you mind if I turn some lights on in here?"

"Go for it." Scottlyn sat back and waited for him to return to his place beside her. She was quiet as he examined the picture in the bright overhead lights.

"Looks like you."

"A little," she agreed. "It's my mom and a twin sister I didn't know she had."

The old pastor met her gaze but held his peace, obviously waiting for her to continue.

"You know that story you told on Sunday morning about God changing your sermon?"

He nodded.

"I think He made you do that for me." Fresh tears tracked her face. "I think I've been an idiot."

He handed the picture back. "You want to talk about it?"

Scottlyn gave him the story and all the emotions that came with it—excitement, confusion, and uncertainty. When she finished, she bit her lip and stared off into space. "Grant and Diana have been telling me to be careful. Grant and I had a huge fight, and now he won't even answer my phone calls." She stared down at the picture. "My stomach's been tied in knots for days. I need to go talk to her, and I'm afraid to, because there's this spot in me that already knows the truth. And I want so much to be wrong."

She looked the old pastor in the eye. "How could something like this happen? Shouldn't God have told me to be careful? How can I call myself a Christian if I'm so easily deceived?"

Pastor Robbins rubbed both hands down his face. "Deliver my soul, O Lord, from lying lips, and from a deceitful tongue."

"Let me guess. A scripture?"

"A very useful verse from Psalms. I'll write it down for you." He faced her with a sympathetic smile. "Scottlyn, you just told me that your stomach's been tied in knots for days. I think God was trying to send you a warning. You're planning a wedding and you buried your father. It's easy to understand that you might have missed it or assigned a different meaning to it. That doesn't make you less of a Christian and neither does being taken advantage of."

He stopped and removed a Bible from the back of the pew. He flipped through a few pages before facing her again. "Do you believe Joshua was a man of God?"

Scottlyn frowned at him. "Yes."

The pastor handed the open Bible to Scottlyn. "I've got to step out and let the missus know I'm going to be a little late for lunch. While I'm on the phone, I want you to read the ninth chapter of Joshua. It's only twenty-six verses. We'll talk about it when I get back. I think you're going to appreciate what it has to say."

He walked out of the room and left her to read. The heading at the top of the chapter read, *The Gibeonites deceive Israel.* Scottlyn sat back, crossed her legs and read. She was nodding her head in agreement long before the pastor returned. She closed the Bible as he slid back into the seat next to her.

"Well?"

"Those Gibeonites were pretty sneaky, and Joshua fell for it."

Pastor Robbins nodded. "The Gibeonites could have won an Oscar for the show they put on that day. They showed up in the Israelite camp in their ragged clothes, packing saddlebags full of moldy bread, and telling a good story about how far they'd traveled. They knew exactly what to say and do to get what they wanted. And Joshua, tired and weary from the battles being fought around him, bought their story. Verse fourteen tells us that Joshua made one crucial mistake that day. He didn't consult the Lord first."

He studied Scottlyn. "We can all be taken in by things that seem to make perfect sense on the outside. That doesn't make us less of a Christian, doesn't mean God doesn't love us or that He's abandoned us. Most of the time it just means we didn't consult the Lord about it first."

Scottlyn raised her hand. "Guilty." She met the preacher's gaze. "How did you get so smart?"

He patted the Bible. "Years and years of study, observation...and consultation."

She squared her shoulders. "I appreciate you taking the time to explain. Why don't you go on and have your lunch? I've got some consulting to do."

~ * ~

Jocelyn opened the door and yanked Andrew inside. "I told you to park down the block."

He pulled her close and lowered his hungry mouth to her pouting lips. His hands clawed at the back of her shirt, slipping a little lower with each accelerated heartbeat.

His groan was laced with a need that matched her own, but she pushed him away. "Not today, Andrew. You can't stay."

"But—"

"Sugar, I don't like it any more than you do, but it's too risky." She stepped around him, peered out the front door, and pushed it closed." I'm supposed to be a grieving widow. Visits from strange men don't support that story."

Andrew drew in a deep, ragged breath. "Babe, you're killing me."

She retrieved a bag from the floor near the door and shoved it against his chest. "Take a look in here. I think you'll revive."

He dumped the contents of the bag onto the small table that stood next to a coat rack and sorted through what she'd collected for him. "Not bad, girlfriend, not bad."

"Told you. This house is a treasure chest just waiting to be claimed, but I can't get too carried away just yet." She reached into her back pocket and handed him a roll of cash. "Here, I found this stuffed in the back of a drawer. There's five hundred dollars there. It won't be missed. I'm pretty sure that if Scottlyn knew it was there, she would have used it when we went shopping. Between the cash and what you can get when you pawn all the small stuff, it should be a couple of thousand."

"You did good." Andrew stuffed the cash into his pocket and raked the loot back into the bag. "Can you spare a cup of coffee before you kick me out?"

"I have a fresh pot in the kitchen."

"In that case, let me run out to the car and grab my thermos."

"Make it snappy and take that bag with you."

Jocelyn watched from the doorway, keeping an eye out for nosey neighbors. She admired Andrew's form as he hurried to the car. *Umm...Umm...Umm, if he only had a brain.*

She was still leering when he came back up the walk.

Andrew's grin turned sly. He nudged the door shut and pulled her close a second time. He threaded his fingers through her hair in a move he knew she couldn't resist. "Just an hour?"

Jocelyn's breath caught in her throat as he pushed her against the wall and molded her body to his. She tilted her head back and gave him access to her throat. "Andrew—"

The door swung open, and the couple separated like guilty teenagers.

Scottlyn stood in the door, arms crossed, eyes wide.

Jocelyn brushed her disheveled hair out of her face. "Scottlyn."

"Hey, Mom...or should I say, Marilyn?"

~ * ~

Scottlyn lifted her chin at the startled look in the other woman's blue eyes. *Please don't let it be true...please don't let it be true.*

"What are you talking about?"

Scottlyn's eyes narrowed to slits. She ignored the man and addressed her *mother*. "Gee, *Mom*. Aren't you going to introduce me to your friend? Is this the one who lives in Tulsa? You know, the one you haven't seen in seventeen years? Amazing how those relationships can just spark right back up."

Marilyn and her friend looked at each other.

"How did you find out?" Marilyn asked.

Scottlyn's shoulders slumped and her eyes closed as the question provided the answer to her fervent prayer. She swallowed back tears. There would be time for those later. Right now, she had to deal with this imposter. Her hand shook as she reached into her pocket and took out the picture. She turned it around so the couple could see.

"I found this in Dad's safe deposit box this morning. It was stuck between two other pictures." She paused and studied the resigned look on the other woman's face. "You aren't even going to try to deny it are you?"

Marilyn shrugged. "Would it do me any good?" She put a hand on her friend's arm. "Go wait in the car, Andrew. You can follow me home."

Andrew looked from one woman to the other. "But, we're just going to leave?"

Marilyn nodded. "We're busted. Just give me a few minutes."

Scottlyn glared at Marilyn as Andrew left. When the door shut behind him, Marilyn turned to Scottlyn and studied her. "You've got brains, kiddo. I like that."

"I'm not concerned about your likes or dislikes." Scottlyn wrapped her fractured heart in layers of determination. She'd lived her whole life without a mother. Why did the idea of returning to that reality sting so much? "Before you leave...permanently...I need to know the truth. What happened to my mother?"

"And a backbone. Trust me, you get that from me, not that worthless sister of mine."

Scottlyn crossed her arms and waited.

"You want the whole story?"

"I want the truth."

Marilyn nodded at the picture. "Twins right? Supposed to share a *special* bond?" She snorted. "Not so much. Jocelyn was always the good girl, always a bit above me, or afraid of me. I never did know which." She leaned in with her hands fisted on her hips. "Do you know she didn't invite me to her wedding, never even told William she had a sister. I guess maybe she was afraid he'd take off if he knew the sort of people she came from. Either that or she was afraid he'd prefer the version with spunk."

"Yeah, I'm sure that was it."

Marilyn chuckled at the sarcasm. "Anyway, once you were born, the tables turned. Jocelyn suddenly decided she needed her sister. She was on the phone every day, crying on my shoulder. She was depressed, she was sad, she was tired...I never did know what she expected me to do for her.

"I had a sweet gig going down in Mexico, and I needed a cover story, so I invited her to tag along. I thought a few days of sun might dry up the water works, you know?"

Marilyn's grin turned to ice. "It was sheer luck that our carry-on bags got switched that day. I realized the mistake when I went to the bathroom, and my motion sick pills weren't in the front pouch. When I came out, they were lining up to board the plane. I saw a couple of uniformed men with a drug dog pull Jocelyn aside for a search, and I knew I'd made the right choice in bringing her along. It was fate, plain and simple."

Scottlyn straightened. "You left your own sister to take the blame for your crime?"

"Well, yeah..."

Scottlyn stared at her. "Tell me where she is. Grant's father is a lawyer, maybe he—"

Marilyn shook her head. "You still don't get it do you? I was just gonna leave her there till she'd learned to appreciate me. I have contacts there, they kept me updated. Jocelyn didn't last twelve months in that Mexican hole. She's been dead for almost seventeen years."

The words hit Scottlyn like a physical blow. She slumped against the wall under their force. The tears came despite her determination to keep them at bay. "What sort of monster are you?"

Marilyn opened the door. "I'm a survivor sweetheart, plain and simple." She took one step toward the door and stopped. "If you want me to leave, I'm going to need to go get my keys."

"Stay right here." Scottlyn's legs trembled as she walked back to her father's bedroom. She gathered up Marilyn's belongings, old and new. When she picked up the new shoes her heart twisted. *I can't believe I argued with Grant over this.* She carried everything back to the door and shoved the whole mess into Marilyn's arms.

"You need to leave, and you need to forget Sabor, Oklahoma, even exists."

"That's it?"

"What more should there be?" Scottlyn asked.

"Just one more thing." Marilyn leaned into Scottlyn's space. "Don't get any crazy ideas about calling the cops." Her smile was evil. "Everything I just told you was nothing more than words between friends. There's no proof." A wave of her hand took in the house. "As for this. The scam went south, no harm no foul. But you need to know that Andrew wouldn't..."

Scottlyn held up a hand to interrupt her. "You can keep your threats to yourself." She met her aunt's cold stare with an equally frigid look. "If I ever see you around me or mine again, I'll use whatever resources I have to have you thrown in jail. That's a promise, not a threat."

Marilyn sneered. "Good luck with that."

Scottlyn shut the door in her face, leaned against it, and held her breath until she heard the noise of both cars leaving. She pulled the picture out of her pocket and studied it. *I don't even know which one is Mom.* She slid to the floor with her back against the door and gave in to the tears.

CHAPTER ELEVEN

Grant looked at the clock as his latest attempt to reach Scottlyn failed. *Almost seven p.m.* He paced up and down the aisle of the small plane. The flight had been pre-cleared to land in Oklahoma City according to customs and border protection procedures, but it seemed to be taking forever to get the plane parked at the private terminal. He sighed when the plane stopped. The engine whine disappeared, and seconds later, the pilot stepped from the cockpit and popped the door open.

Grant bounded for the opening but turned at the top of the steps and nodded at his new friend. "Thanks!"

He took the steps two at a time and sprinted for the overnight parking garage, phone held to his ear as he ran. *No answer.* "Scottie, where are you?"

He punched in Diana's number instead.

"Grant, thank goodness."

The tension in her voice stopped Grant in his tracks. "What's wrong?"

"I'm not exactly sure. Scottlyn came home a couple of hours ago. I could tell she'd been crying. I'm more than a little worried about her. I've never seen her like this...and she won't talk to me. She helped Mercie with her dinner, ignored her own plate, and now she's taking care of Mercie's bath. Routine chores, but she's going about them with the animation of a robot."

Grant shifted back into high gear. "I don't know if what I found is going to help that mood, but I'll be there in an hour."

~ * ~

"Mommy don't cry."

Scottlyn blinked as she tucked the towel around Mercie, lifted her off the floor, and carried her daughter to her room. "What?"

Mercie framed her mother's face with her small hands and leaned in to kiss each cheek. She straightened up and wiped at her mouth. "Tears are yucky."

Had she been crying? *Maybe a better question is, when will I stop?* She bundled the child close and gulped a breath. The fragrances of soap and baby shampoo soothed her soul. Her arms tightened.

This child would never wonder who her mother was or lie awake at night trying to remember the details of her absent mother's face. With God's help and her own determination, Mercie would always know that she was loved above life itself.

You are loved, daughter. Don't forget that.

Scottlyn sucked in another breath as the soft words caressed her heart. *Loved?* She bit her lip.

Grant loves you. Diana loves you.

"And Mercie loves me," she whispered in concert with the voice speaking to her soul.

And I love you most of all.

"Mommy, I'm squished."

Scottlyn relaxed her grip. "I'm sorry, baby." She set the child on the edge of the bed, retrieved a comb, and prepared to attack the tangled mess of baby-fine hair. Straight now instead of curly. Her daughter's hair seemed to get straighter with every inch it grew.

"I miss your curls."

Mercie squirmed. "Curls are for babies. Ouch!"

"Almost done." Scottlyn gave the blonde hair a final pass with the comb and helped Mercie slip into her pj's.

"Grandma Diana said something about a bedtime story. Why don't you run find her and tell her you're ready?"

"OK." Mercie sprinted for the door, slid to a stop, and turned at the threshold. "You're the bestest mommy in the world."

Scottlyn swallowed a sob and forced a smile. "Do you really think so?"

Mercie nodded and bolted from the room.

Scottlyn picked up dirty clothes and the damp towel and tidied Mercie's bedroom and the bathroom. She flipped off the lights, sat on her bed, and scooted up to the headboard. She drew up her knees, wrapped her arms around them, and lowered her head.

"Father I know You love me most of all. You've blessed me. You've surrounded me with people who love me." *Jocelyn didn't last twelve months in that Mexican hole.* The words and the cruelty with which they'd been delivered raised goose bumps on Scottlyn's arms. "This is so hard. I'm sorry if I'm being greedy, but please help me find a way to make this better."

~ * ~

Grant's car screeched to a halt in Diana's drive. He'd made the sixty-minute drive from the airport in fifty. He threw the seatbelt aside and hurried to the door. The need to get to Scottlyn drove protocol from his mind. He caught himself just before he rushed through the door without even a knock and cracked it open instead.

"Diana?"

"Grant!"

The door was yanked out of his hand, and a tiny blonde missile launched into his arms. Kisses rained on his face as Mercie snuggled into his arms. "I missed your face!"

Mercie never failed to lighten his heart. *What did I ever do before she and Scottlyn became a part of my life?* Grant chuckled in spite of the urgency of his errand. "My face has only been gone for two days, goofy girl." He hugged her close for a few seconds before setting her on her feet. "Where's Mom?"

Mercie frowned up at him. "In her room. She has another boo-boo heart."

Grant looked to Diana for a translation. "The day of the funeral Scottlyn told her she was crying because her heart hurt."

He nodded. "Gotcha'."

Mercie grabbed his hand and tugged. "Come tuck me in."

Grant stooped down. "I need to talk to your mommy first. Can you stay here with Grandma Diana for a while? I promise I won't leave before I tuck you in. I'll even throw in an extra story."

Mercie threw her arms around his neck a second time. "You're gonna be my bestest daddy!"

Oh, squirt, I hope so. Grant untangled himself and kissed her nose. "I'll be back in a little bit." He followed the hallway down to the connected bedrooms Mercie and Scottlyn occupied. The door to Mercie's was closed, and no light glowed from beneath it. He raised his hand to knock on Scottlyn's, but the unlatched door opened at his touch. The sound of soft crying twisted his heart and drove him to Scottlyn's side.

He sat on the edge of the bed and gathered his fiancée into his arms. "I'm here, Scottie."

Scottlyn melted against him and snuggled her face into the crook of his neck. "Oh, Grant, I'm so sorry. I was afraid I'd lost you too."

"Not possible."

She continued as if she hadn't heard him. "I didn't mean to make you mad."

He held her tighter. "Sweetheart, I was never mad at you, just concerned for you."

"And I should have listened. That woman...Mom's dead."

How does she...? He held his questions and rocked her as she dissolved into a fresh torrent of tears. When the flood dwindled to a trickle, he held her away a little and stared into her face, thankful for the little bit of light spilling in from the hall.

"We're going to get through this, OK? I'm here, and I'm always going to be here. I know things feel pretty bleak right now, but they'll get better. You need to believe that."

She sniffed, plucked a tissue from the bedside table, and mopped her face before she blew her nose. "It's so hard."

He framed her face in his hands. "I know." He shifted, and the envelope in his pocket crackled, reminding him of its presence and the knowledge Scottlyn wasn't supposed to have just yet.

"Scoot over, we need to talk." They maneuvered until they both sat propped against the headboard. Grant took her hand. "I took a little trip today...well, yesterday and today. I flew down to Cozumel to check out Jocelyn's story."

Scottlyn bowed her head. "Did you find anything?"

"Just verification of what you've already learned." He tugged her hand, waiting until she met his gaze. "How did you figure out that your mom is dead?"

Scottlyn leaned over, switched on the bedside lamp, and picked up a picture. She studied it for a second before passing it over to him. "I found this in Dad's safe deposit box this morning."

Grant whistled as the pieces fell into place. "Twins? I didn't see that coming."

"I'm pretty sure Dad never knew either. Marilyn said Mom never told him she had a sister and this picture was stuck between two others." Scottlyn shared the details of her confrontation with her aunt. "She a vicious, cruel woman. I can't believe she just left Mom there and came home like nothing happened."

"Some people are just born cross-wired. I know that doesn't help, but I'm glad you sent her packing."

He removed the paperwork from his pocket. "I found your mother's death certificate..."

Scottlyn's sob stopped him, and he paused to see if the tears were making a return appearance. Instead, she drew in a shuddering breath and waited for him to finish.

"And I found an envelope with your name on it."

~ * ~

My dearest baby girl, I saw a calendar in the infirmary today and realized you just celebrated your second birthday. It broke my heart to know that you celebrated without me. It breaks my heart to know that you will celebrate them all without me.

Scottlyn, I don't know if you will ever see this letter. I'm praying that someday, once you're old enough to understand, some twist of fate or blessing will bring it to your hand.

Oh, baby, I miss you. Your sweet toothless smiles, your stumbling attempts to walk. The memory of those things is what keeps me going in this horrible place...at least it has until now.

I know you are going to grow up with questions your father can't answer. He can't answer because he doesn't know. The fact that I left without telling him anything about the trip haunts me every day.

Marilyn convinced me that she was in trouble. That no one could know our plans. She told me that she just needed a week to work things out. That while she did that I could get some rest and find my smile once more.

She betrayed me. She was jealous of what I had, of the life I was building. She never wanted it for herself, she just didn't want me to have it either. I had no idea she would go to such lengths to destroy my life.

I know she'll never share what happened with you or William, and now...now it doesn't really matter. Scottlyn, if you ever meet this woman, please stay far, far away from her. She is wicked to the core. She stole my future.

I'm dying. Some bug I picked up in this hole. I want you to know that I fought it, hoping, praying that some miracle would restore my health and bring me home. That's not going to happen.

I loved you. I never left you willingly. You held my heart in your tiny hands from the moment you were born. I know you are going to grow up so much wiser and stronger than I ever was.

The one bright spot in this whole ordeal is that I've accepted Christ into my life. I know He'll reach out to you as well when the time is right. This isn't goodbye.

I'm waiting to hold you in my arms again.

Love, Mommy

The letter fell from Scottlyn's trembling fingers. The words ripped her heart open and soothed the wound all at the same time. "She loved me, she didn't abandon me."

She turned into the arms of the man who loved her enough to find this letter and bring her peace. "Oh,

Grant, she loved me."

EPILOGUE

Fifty-eight days later

The bride room of Sabor's Faith Tabernacle bustled with activity as three females vied for the mirror at the same time.

"Mercie, hold still," Scottlyn scolded.

"I want to get married, Mommy."

"So do I, and I'd like for both of us to look our best." She tightened the pink bow in Mercie's hair.

Mercie spun away and faced Diana. "Am I bootiful?"

Diana cupped her chin. "More than."

Scottlyn stooped down next to her daughter. "I have one more thing to make it perfect. Close your eyes and hold out your hands."

Mercie did as she was told, but she bounced in her satin slippers.

Scottlyn laid a small box in her hands. "OK."

Mercie opened her eyes. "A present?" She looked up.

"It's a wedding gift for *bootiful* little girls. Take out the card and I'll help you read it."

The three-year-old ripped the card from the box and held it up to her mother. "Read it...read it..."

Miss Mercie, Happy wedding day. Will you be my little girl forever? I love you, Daddy.

Mercie giggled. "Grant..."

Scottlyn frowned down at her. "Who?"

"I mean Daddy." Her eyes went round when she opened the box. Small gold hoops rested on the black velvet inside. She stroked them with a finger. "Can I wear them?"

"Of course." Scottlyn stooped, removed Mercie's favorite pink studs, and replaced them with the hoops.

Mercie stared into the mirror, turning her head back and forth.

"That was sweet," Diana said.

"Grant picked them out last week. He wanted her to have something that would last."

"He's a good man. You're very lucky."

Scottlyn shook her head. "Luck had nothing to do with it. I'm blessed beyond measure."

The women looked up at a knock on the door and an anonymous voice. "You ladies ready?"

Scottlyn looked at the surrogate mother who would give her away and the daughter ready to fling pink rose petals in her path. "Let's do this."

At the entry to the auditorium, she joined hands with Diana. The music changed, and Scottlyn's breath caught in her throat when Grant looked up. She saw every answer she ever needed in her groom's eyes.

Her home with Diana, the saving grace of an awesome God, her precious daughter, the new hope that she would see her mother again, the promise of the future she saw on Grant's face. No matter how she sliced it, looked at it, or spelled it, every smidge of her life truly was all about Mercie.

ABOUT THE AUTHOR

Sharon Srock went from science fiction to Christian fiction at slightly less than warp speed. Twenty-five years ago, she cut her writer's teeth on Star Trek fiction. Today, she writes inspirational stories that focus on ordinary women and their extraordinary faith. Sharon lives in the middle of nowhere Oklahoma with her husband and three very large dogs. When she isn't writing you can find her cuddled up with a good book, baking something interesting in the kitchen, or exploring a beach on vacation. She hasn't quite figured out how to do all three at the same time.

Connect with her here:

Blog: http://www.sharonsrock.com

Facebook: http://www.facebook.com/SharonSrock#!/Sharon Srock

Goodreads: http://www.goodreads.com/author/show/64487 89.Sharon_Srock

Sign up for her quarterly newsletter from the blog or Facebook page.